HAMPSHIRE & ISLE OF WIGHT GHOST TALES

HAMPSHIRE & ISLE OF WIGHT GHOST TALES

MICHAEL O'LEARY

To Paul and Jacqueline Eldridge

Paul and Jacqueline first heard me tell stories in Southampton General Hospital, when one of their children was a patient there, back in the 1990s. Then, as their kids grew up, they came to many of my Halloween storytelling sessions. After the children were no longer children, and had flown the nest, Paul and Jacqueline, both builders, appeared like angels to help with a major problem I had with my house. Friends through storytelling – stories and practicality; I love that!

First published 2016

The History Press
The Mill, Brimscombe Port
Stroud, Gloucestershire, GL5 2QG
www.thehistorypress.co.uk

© Michael O'Leary, 2016
Illustrations © Ruth O'Leary, 2016

British Library Cataloguing in Publication Data.
A catalogue record for this book is available from the British Library.

ISBN 978 0 7509 6366 4

Typesetting and origination by The History Press
Printed and bound by CPI Group (UK) Ltd

CONTENTS

Acknowledgements

Thanks to Rosie Sutcliffe, my walking companion, for helping me to explore many of the areas in this book. My competitive streak tells me that one day I'll find a footpath that Rosie doesn't already know, but it hasn't happened yet!

Thanks to Jenny Barnard for drawing my attention to the Minstead Cat people, and for many a walk, and a few drinks, shared with her and Roy.

Thanks to Karl Bell for giving me food for thought about the nature of ghost stories.

Thanks to Kath Watkins of www.jigfoot.com for sharing information about Alice Gillington and her time in the New Forest.

Thanks to Chris Westcott, wild woodland woman of www.threecopse.co.uk for suggesting that I visit Deadwoman's Gate. I am sorry that Chris is so lacking in appreciation of my wonderful bagpipe playing that she insists on threatening me with various lethal woodland implements when I play a sweet melody.

Thanks to Scott Pritchard, caretaker extraordinaire, for a conversation about haunted school buildings. Thanks to Sheila Jemima for her story about Winkle Street.

Thanks to my daughter, Ruth O'Leary, for her appropriately quirky internal illustrations and thank you to Katherine Soutar for her striking front cover.

Thanks to Geoff the postie, Charlie the Cork Head, Jim Privett, and all the people I've listened to and talked with, in pubs and lanes and paths and places.

Thank you, also, to 'Old Nan', who may, or may not, exist.

INTRODUCTION

One evening I stood in the fifteenth-century Square Tower in Portsmouth – telling ghost stories. The Square Tower is in old Point, also known as Spice Island; the oldest part of Pompey and dripping with the salt water of maritime ghost stories. Point is where the ghost of murdered Commander Buster Crabbe flip flaps in his flippers and frogman suit along the foreshore; this is where you might wake up next to the corpse of an eighteenth-century sailor, his head bound up with a bloody handkerchief; this was the launching pad from where the wraith of a pregnant young woman who had sold her soul to the Devil for the sake of revenge, rocketed away in a screaming trajectory to the ship of her faithless and exploitative lover, from where she dragged him into the sea and down to hell.

I told the story of Jack the Painter, the revolutionary who was strung up outside the dockyard gates, and whose body was gibbeted out on Blockhouse Point – whose ghost walks old Pompey with rattling bones and chattering teeth.

When I'd finished, and the only people left in the tower were me and the chap waiting to lock up, there was a big bump from upstairs. The young man thought he'd better check the toilets again in case he locked anyone in for the night; he did so rather nervously, and then we both legged it. Ghost stories have that effect on you, and I was ready to believe that the ghost of Jack the Painter really was about to come clattering down the stairs and take a few bites out of my throat. I'd scared myself!

But then ghost stories tell as much about us as they do about ghosts – whatever ghosts may be. Karl Bell, studying the 'hauntology' (Jacques Derrida's glorious word to describe the way our assumptions, feelings and thoughts about the past and the future bleed into our perception of the immediate present) of Portsmouth, wrote about the relationship between people and their perceptions of ghosts; and it is clear how ghost stories adapt, morph and merge with the way our lives are structured and lived at any point in history. So Karl doesn't just chase ghosts around Portsmouth, he looks at the historical and cultural backgrounds of the stories, and this is what illuminates our lives and history.

Mind you, I'm attempting no such depth here, and given that my belated academic career culminated in a 2:2 in Geography, it's probably just as well. I'm just telling tales. Aha – but then what assumptions am I unconsciously making? I'll leave that for the reader to interpret.

When I wrote *Hampshire and Isle of Wight Folk Tales* half the stories turned out to be ghost stories, including the story of Jack the Painter, so I can't bung that one into this book! Similarly I can't include some of the more famous Hampshire ghost stories, such as the midnight toilings of the ghost of the rector of Vernham Dean, or the various appearances of a blood-soaked Rufus the Red, or the hideous ghost of the executed child murderer, Michael Morey, on the Isle of Wight – as I have already told them – but Hampshire and the Island are stuffed with a lot more ghost stories than I included in that particular book.

They're urban, they're rural, they're maritime, they're land-locked, they are good, bad, ugly and beautiful. They reflect the people. And before any keeper of the county's folklore – one who would fossilise the fragments of communal memory and transmission into the proper and the improper, the correct and the incorrect – whacks me over the head with a dictionary of folklore, I confess that I have been guilty of applying my own imagination to these stories. Just a bit.

Michael O'Leary
2016

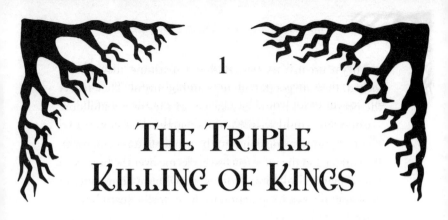

1

THE TRIPLE
KILLING OF KINGS

I t's not that I'm cynical about ghosts in a stereotypical way; I'm not someone who says, 'Bah humbug' and then, inevitably, gets visited by a spook. I'm perfectly aware that because so much is defined by our own perception, 'reality' can become quite a fluid concept.

I am, however, a bit of an empiricist and when I search for the simplest rational explanation, according to the principles of Occam's razor, I don't think that I'm lessening the wonder of things; rather the opposite. Searching for a supernatural explanation is invariably something that lessens wonder; something that is almost banal. So, if bumps in the night are explained by the presence of a malignant poltergeist, rather than movements of the earth caused by the presence of mine shafts, or eddies and currents in the air caused by a change in the weather, there is less wonder, and a sort of self-centred arrogance that explains everything around human agency.

So, when sitting comfortably in the front bar of the Junction Inn, Southampton, with Andrew telling me about ghostly experiences in the New Forest, I remained polite and seemingly interested, but internally I felt a bit of a cringe, the feeling that I've often had when people find out that I earn my living as a storyteller, and seem to think that I'll therefore be interested in their 'paranormal' experiences. I'm glad I didn't express my scepticism now, though, because Andrew's subsequent death would have given me a burden of guilt.

Mind you, Andrew didn't announce that he was going to tell me a ghost story; we began by just chatting about walks in the New Forest – and the fact that the *New* Forest is very old. Of course the Forest (locally it's always just known as 'the Forest', in the same way that the Isle of Wight is just known as 'the Island') got its name from the Normans – and it is only new in the sense that William the Bastard, later to be known as William the Conqueror (though no doubt you have to be the one in order to be the other), made it his own personal hunting ground. It feels old, and some of the parts of the Forest that possess a particular feeling of archaism are not wooded – but are the open, boggy parts: the valley mires. The New Forest, and I do love its pre-Norman name 'Ytene', has 75 per cent of Europe's valley mires, a specific kind of peat bog, although many a car-bound visitor doesn't get to see them.

Andrew had been walking that day in the area around White Moor, near Emery Down, and he probably super-imposed his own depression onto the landscape. He had recently 'been through a messy divorce' – a phrase I put into inverted commas not just because it's a cliché, though a perfectly effective one, but because Andrew tended to trot it out when apologising for his gloominess. It meant that he didn't have to start explaining anything else; his own culpability for the divorce, details and feelings, guilt and betrayal, the way he missed his family – and probably the loss of a certain sort of male status. Things that might prove something of a dampener in a pub conversation.

Andrew had been walking through an area of massive beech trees, many of which had dropped whole limbs after recent storms, and the lordly but battered beeches, the holly trees between them, the deer-scabbed stumps, the occasional gnarled old oaks, set a scene that was full of strange, primeval faces, twisted expressions and crooked fingers. He came to a sudden edge to both the trees and the leaf and beech-nut strewn forest floor, and found himself gazing out over a valley mire. He stopped there – he wasn't wearing his wellies – and remarked to himself that you don't have to be on Dartmoor to come across a Grimpen Mire. It was a bit like a 1960s Hammer horror film of *The Hound of the Baskervilles*; you'd imagine someone had been using dry ice to raise the low mist that was swirling over the peat bog. Out of that mist, in the centre of the bog, rising stark and white, was a large silver birch tree – large for a silver birch anyway. It was a beautiful scene, though not a bright and cheery one, and Andrew felt something that he found hard to describe to me: 'Not exactly hostility, because I felt that I was meant to be there, but something that didn't mean me any good.'

'It gets a bit like that,' I waffled, 'parts of the Forest can be quite eerie …'

'No, no,' said Andrew, and I suddenly realised he was trying to describe something that was really quite important to him, 'I was scared, really scared, but it wasn't like being spooked out. I felt really glum, too. Then – I saw something …'

Now, I work as a storyteller, and I've heard a lot of other professional storytellers. They have learned the techniques that make a story effective, when a pause or a sudden phrase can startle an audience; they wait for that polished, proudly produced combination of words to make its impact on the listeners, whilst they look at their audience in a meaningful and knowing manner. But in the end, the real power of storytelling doesn't come out of prancing professionalism; when it all comes down to dust, as it will and as it must, the telling of a story is informed by the content of the story – and the extent to which the storyteller feels it in his, or her, bones.

'Then – I saw something …'

I went cold when he said that; the clinking glasses, the chatter, the laughter and banter faded away – I was completely focused on Andrew's story – it was me standing at the tree line on the edge of White Moor, looking over the ground mist to a stark, white skeletal silver birch tree.

'I saw a figure, standing by the tree, holding up both hands, and it looked like he had a knife in one hand, and a cord, or rope, or something, hanging from the other hand.'

'What was it?'

'I don't know – the figure was there, and then it wasn't there. It didn't disappear – just it was there, and then it wasn't.'

I rather lamely said something about the mind and the eyes playing tricks – then realised that I was rather insulting him – so finished by saying something about 'a good story'.

It stuck with me, though; in fact the image insinuated itself into my mind to such an extent that, as I cycled home to Northam, my old riverside part of Southampton, along the wooden causeway that skirts the edge of the estuarine River Itchen, I kept seeing images of the figure standing in the estuary mud.

Over the next few days it niggled at me. A cord and a knife. A peat bog. There was something familiar about it all. And I kept seeing the silver birch and the figure.

It was Andrew who told me, though, and that was during the next time I bumped into him in the Junction. He'd been doing his research.

'It's the triple killing of kings.'

Now, that was it. I remember reading about the Lindow Man – the body found in a bog in Cheshire. A few of these bodies had been found, preserved in bogs throughout Europe, and they were thought to be ritualistic killings – overkill, really; they'd had their throats cut, they'd received a blow to the head, and they'd been strangled. Triple killing.

'Well, you like stories,' said Andrew, 'it's there in the old stories – you only have to look at Wikipedia. There are stories about Merlin prophesying his own death; it's in old Irish stories, Norse stories about Odin – the lot. The king is no good anymore, because the crops have failed, or there have been disasters, or something, and he pays the price: he gets the chop three times.'

'Well, you never said you saw all that.'

'No, but the figure with the cord and the knife; he's the killer. I know it, I've been back.'

Andrew had been back to White Moor several times. He'd seen the figure again.

I began to feel a bit impatient. It was interesting enough at first; but now it was getting obsessive.

'Well, it's a good thing you're not a king, then,' I said, 'I don't s'pose you'd let the harvest fail.'

'Aren't I?'

I didn't know what he meant by that.

Mind you, the Forest did kill kings. The death of Rufus is the classic example. The Rufus Stone, near Canterton Glen in the Forest, is said to mark the spot where Rufus the Red, son and heir to William the Conqueror, was killed by an arrow fired by Walter Tyrrell. This was passed off as a hunting accident, but was probably an assassination. However, there are lots of stories and theories that have grown up about it being some sort of a sacrificial killing – Rufus having to atone for poor harvests. It's something that I'd been interested in, and I'd read that historians tended to think that the killing didn't take place at Canterton Glen at all, but near Beaulieu, a place many miles south of the Rufus Stone. My own theory, entirely unsupported by any evidence, is that the historical story had superimposed itself onto something much older – a story of death and sacrifice. To me, Canterton Glen, in spite of the A31 dual carriageway that thunders through it, has always seemed an eerie place; and Canterton, Cantwaratun in Old English, means farm of the Kentish men, and Kentish men doesn't necessarily mean men from Kent; it means the 'other' people, the strange ones. Of course, Canterton Glen isn't White Moor, but they both have that feeling about them, and they're not so far apart.

I continued to be haunted by the story, although I rather dreaded seeing Andrew again; because he'd gotten so monomaniacal about it all – and I wondered a little bit if he'd actually looked up all this stuff about the triple killing of kings before he'd supposedly seen the ghost on White Moor.

I must admit, though, I went there myself. It was just part of a walk – I didn't particularly intend to check it out.

Honest. I saw a silver birch in the valley mire – it wasn't quite as central as I'd imagined, but probably I was just looking from a different angle. I didn't see any figure, though, but I did feel something. That great writer about the countryside, Brian Vesey-Fitzgerald, once wrote about a feeling of hostility that sometimes, just sometimes, can be felt from the Forest – but then given Andrew's story, it was hardly surprising that I should feel it on the edge of White Moor.

In the end, though, Andrew's death had nothing to do with valley mires, or White Moor, or Iron Age rituals.

It was awful to hear about it. I'd cycled to the Junction, down the wooden causeway by the river, thinking about another king. Sir Henry Englefield wrote, in 1805, about King Canute sitting on his throne in the 'black and oozy bed of the Itchen at Northam' to show his courtiers that no one had the power to gainsay the word of God and hold back the tide; though another story said he buried his enemies up to their necks there, and watched them drown as the tide came in.

Anyway, it was Tracy at the pub who told me about Andrew's death.

'He was killed outright,' she said. 'I think he was going to Bournemouth or somewhere; he skidded off the road and hit a tree.'

'Anyone else involved?'

'No – they think he had a heart attack, so then he crashed, and then the car caught fire. Three things made pretty sure he was gone.'

'Where did this happen?'

'On the A31 – where it goes through the Forest – you know, near the sign to the Rufus Stone.'

Of course, as I cycled home, with a few pints inside me that had been consumed in a somewhat maudlin fashion,

there should have been no problem with the Itchen causeway – it wasn't as if it was White Moor, or Canterton Glen,
or anywhere in the Forest.

But I didn't fancy it. The tide was out, and I didn't want
to look at all that mud. I ignored the causeway, and took the
longer route home along the road.

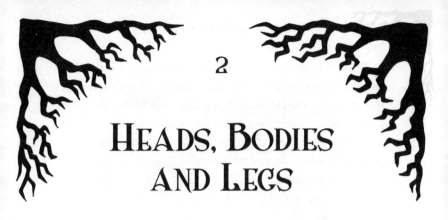

2

HEADS, BODIES AND LEGS

I f ever there was an organisation that suffers from being stereotyped, it's the Women's Institute. There was always the jam and cake making stereotype and then, to upset that, along came the naked calendar stereotype, assisted by *Calendar Girls*, a film which rather unfairly portrayed the WI as being originally, rather stuffily, opposed to the calendar; whereas the organisation was, in fact, supportive. Both stereotypes contain truth, of course, but – as stereotypes tend to be – they are more than a little condescending: a condescension that is somewhat metropolitan. Of course the WI is made up from a wide variety of women, women with all sorts of attitudes and political viewpoints, and, as Tony Blair discovered when he tried to use them to deliver a party political speech in 2000, they will not be used or patronised.

One of the things that I have discovered about the WI, no doubt due to the commitment to community that lies at its heart, is that many of its members have a lot of knowledge of, and interest in, their own localities, and often carry stories that might otherwise be forgotten. I love being hired as a speaker – storyteller – by WI groups, because I always get stories back. I finish, and someone tells me a local story, and my story-stealing antennae goes into overdrive.

When I have researched Hampshire stories I often find that the latest book, or web page, simply regurgitates the information culled from the book that went before, the book before having done the same thing, and so on; the written transmission of these stories being nothing more than a lazy plagiarism of books and websites; with no flesh and blood word of mouth, and no real knowledge of the localities. At the root of this plagiarism, however, lies a truly original book, a book which is often not given any attribution, and that wondrous book is called *It Happened in Hampshire*. It was compiled and arranged by Winifred G. Beddington and Elsa B. Christy, and it was published by the Hampshire Federation of Women's Institutes in 1936.

In the foreword, Beddington and Christy write: 'We have […] tried, when possible, to retain the wording in which they [the information] reached us.' In other words, many of their sources are from the spoken word. In the chapter titled 'Legends, Stories and Sayings', they relate a story about a haunted cottage, which they got from a member of the WI who lived in the village of Braishfield.

Many years ago it appears that a lady of some means was in fear of her accumulated wealth being forcibly taken from her. She therefore decided to conceal it where prying eyes could not find it, and she selected a spot near an isolated cottage in the village. Soon after she became ill, was taken to the infirmary and died. It is now believed that she still wanders round the place of her hidden wealth, jealous that someone else should find and enjoy it. She is continually seen, and more frequently heard, knocking at the door of the cottage and making other weird noises …

… One man, now living, said he saw her 'a sittin' on the wicket and me 'air fair pushed me 'at off me 'ead'.

The thing with stories though is that they don't remain safely on the printed page – that's just an interlude in the progression of the story – the printed word freezes it, but only temporarily.

You see, I heard more about this story, but from a completely different source. I'll tell you about that source later, when it becomes relevant, but first I'll tell you about that cottage several decades after it got a mention in *It Happened in Hampshire*.

We need to travel backward in time to the 1960s. The process of suburbanisation, a change in the nature of the countryside that was more than physical, was well underway, and, as social and technological processes tend to do, it was accelerating.

That cottage in Braishfield had gone to rack and ruin – no one wanted to live in it because of the ghost of that terrible old woman; forever banging on the door, blowing out the fire, moaning and complaining, tut-tutting, and stamping on the creakiest of the floorboards. The last owner had died during the war, and given that his only beneficiary was a relative who had emigrated to Canada long ago, the cottage stood empty, slowly disintegrating.

In the 1960s, however, someone got hold of it (don't ask me about how legal matters of ownership take place) and given that Braishfield was well into the process of becoming a dormitory village for Southampton and Winchester, they were having it 'done up'. The ghost story was just silly, of course, and what important 'money man' was ever going to come across something as inconsequential as a book by the WI.

A group of men were working on it – brickies, chippies, plasterers, electricians, plumbers. It so happened that they'd all come up from Southampton, except for one. He'd got the train from Portsmouth to Southampton, from where they'd given him a lift. In Hampshire, Portsmouth is popularly known, for a variety of reasons, as Pompey. If you're not familiar with the nuances of Hampshire, Pompey people are well known for their erudition, their love of a good, vigorous debate, and their attention to the finer aspects of detail whilst making debating points.

These men had finished work for the day, and repaired to the local hostelry for a pint or three. A debate had arisen over some detail of theology or politics, possibly relating to the relative fortunes of Portsmouth and Southampton FC, and the vigour and passion of the debate was such that chairs flew around the pub, and the gentleman from Pompey found himself being pitched over the bar. The Southampton contingent then drove off pissed as newts (why are newts considered to be exemplars of intoxication?), leaving the Pompey man bruised, boozed-up, and stranded in Braishfield. As the locals emerged from hiding, he staggered off down the street and, wondering what to do, concluded that he might as well spend the night in the cottage.

He was too drunk to light a fire, so he wrapped himself in a dustsheet and lay on the floor in front of the fireplace.

It is hard to wake someone when they've had too much to drink, so it took quite a noise to wake him up. The noise was provided by a terrible shriek that emanated from the chimney, a clattering and banging, followed by a great shower of damp, congealed soot, and the descent down the chimney of a spindly, veiny, blotchy pair of legs; both of which proceeded to leap and caper round the room – one leg around another – because that's all there was – two separate legs – no body being present at all, let alone a head.

The Pompey man gazed blearily at the legs, but a brain after a skinful isn't given to considering a situation and deciding that fear induced by the supernatural is the appropriate response.

'What the f*** is this?' said the Pompey man.

'Wash your dirty mouth out, young man,' screamed a voice from the chimney, 'and have a bit of decency; don't go looking at my lovely legs.'

'Lllegs,' mumbled the Pompey man, who could see a lot more than two legs capering around the room, 'f*** off, legs.'

'Filthy man, filthy man,' screeched the voice from the chimney, and there was more crashing and banging, before down the chimney tumbled a torso, most decently attired in a long, black dress. The torso dragged itself across the floor by its hands and lifted itself onto the legs, which were now decently covered by the dress.

The Pompey man thought that this was all a bit much, so lowered his head again and recommenced snoring.

'Thief, thief! You're after my treasure, I know you are,' screamed the voice from the chimney, and the word 'treasure' connected with something in the Pompey man's brain.

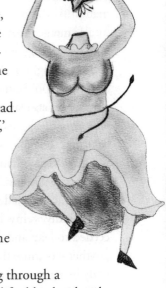

'Treasure?' he mumbled, lifting his head.

'Get away from my treasure you thief,' screamed the spectre's head as it came tumbling down the chimney to be picked up by the hands and stuck roughly onto the neck, 'get away from my treasure!' This was all beyond the Pompey man's comprehension, so he started snoring again.

Then the dawn sunshine was shining through a broken window, and the Pompey man lifted his head and opened a bleary eye. The old woman was sitting on a pile of cement sacks by the door.

'You've broken the spell; you've set me free,' she said with a sudden smile that changed the look of her face altogether.

He stared at her uncomprehendingly.

'When I was young, I was in love,' she said, 'but he upped and left me for a loose woman who came by with the fair.'

'Bastard,' said the Pompey man, who now more fully comprehended the strangeness of the situation and thought that an expression of disapproval might be appropriate.

'From then on,' continued the woman, 'I turned mean. I hoarded and hoarded my money; and I couldn't bear the thought of anyone getting their hands on it.'

'Money …' thought the Pompey man.

'After I died, I was tied to this cottage by my money – that is, unless someone could stay the night without fear. It wasn't going to be a handsome prince, but you'll do – you've set me free.'

'Money?' muttered the Pompey man. 'Where's the money?'

'It's out in the garden,' she called in a fading voice, 'buried under the apple tree – I don't need it anymore – I'm free …' after which she turned into what seemed like a whirlwind of soot, and disappeared up the chimney with a roar like the ten thousand flapping wings of a murmuration of starlings.

The Pompey man dug the treasure up with a shovel used for slinging sand and cement into the mixer – only a Pompey man could dig a hole with a shovel – and he found the treasure chest. When he levered it open his eyes glittered as much as the old gold coins in the morning sunlight.

Well, the long and the short of it is, he hid the box, he retrieved it later, and he brought it back to Pompey.

In a folk story, that would be the end of things. It would be Jack, the youngest of three sons, who finds the treasure, he would be rich, he'd use the treasure well, and that would be the end of the story. But, in all practicality, what do you do with a chest full of old gold coins? Gold coins that shouldn't be in your possession. You can't just take them to a bank and say, 'Give me some money please', and claim entitlement on the say-so of a ghost.

The Pompey man had to find someone who would give him some money for something acquired in a less than legal manner, and this meant finding a 'fence'.

This really brought him into some rather bad company, but it seemed to be a milieu in which he could carve out quite a place for himself. As the money disappeared – and it didn't take long for it to run between his fingers – he needed more, and his place in the company in which he found himself seemed to require the use of sawn-off shotguns and (this being the '60s) stockings over the head.

If one averages out the earnings of a life of crime into a weekly wage, it really never can be much, particularly because of long and frequent periods of incarceration; though these periods do provide free board and lodging.

It is in prison, by the way, that I met the Pompey man, and completed the story begun in a book produced by two members of the WI. I'd better explain.

I used to tell stories in various HM prisons – sometimes I was storytelling for the children of prisoners during visiting times, and sometimes I was working with prisoners who were making recordings of stories they could send to their children. It was during a visit to Wormwood Scrubs that I met the gentleman in question. I asked his permission to relate the story, though he didn't want me to give his name because he was never prosecuted for the removal of that chest of gold coins from the cottage in Braishfield.

I am, however, very serious about the ethical transmission of folklore and stories, and I would never dream of using sources that were less than honest and trustworthy. I have never met the two ladies of the WI, who wrote that wonderful book back in 1936, but I'm absolutely certain that they were honest and trustworthy, and would never dream of making anything up.

3

THE APPLE
TREE MAN

First thing in the morning we used to 'switch the greens'.
This was in 1977 when I was a greenkeeper. The greens
would be covered in a blanket of dew, and this could
incubate fusarium disease and fairy rings. The word 'disease'
makes it sound very sinister, but it's only called a disease because
it's something not wanted by golfers – an innocuous fungus –
and fairy rings, as the name implies, are surely beautiful.

But golfers want the greens to be green – an unblemished,
regular, livid green desert – so we'd be there at seven thirty in
the morning with our long fibreglass rods, swishing semicir-
cles on the grass, which would transform from dewy silver
to bright green as we swished the long, flexible rods over the
surface. It was very therapeutic. Then at nine o'clock – time
for a tea break – the van would arrive, honking furiously,
from Stainer's bakery in Bishops Waltham, and the smell of
freshly baked lardy cake would drift across the greens and
fairways, and we'd be ready for a brew up.

Jim Privett thought the sight of us switching the greens
was hilarious. The land had only recently become a golf
course, indeed when I first went to work there it was still
under construction, and it used to be a farm. Jim, who was
ninety-six years old, had worked on that land all his life;

though it didn't seem to trouble him seeing it being turned into a golf course. It troubled me – and I was part of the process – but I suppose a job is a job.

Jim had been exempted from military service during the First World War, because agriculture was a vital industry. I have a feeling that not everyone was really so eager to rush off and do their patriotic duty – and that was the one event that might have taken him away from Hampshire. His world was – geographically – a small one. To him, Bishops Waltham was 'sin city' where all sorts of stuff went on – and probably it did – and as for Southampton and Portsmouth, well, they were far away metropolises. The centre of his world was Sandy Lane, that sunken lane that snaked from the Botley Road to Waltham Chase. I don't mean to infer that Jim's world was small in every way, because we all have approximately the same size brain, so surely we interpret our physical surroundings and experience according to our own consciousness and perception. In days when aeroplanes can whisk us off to other countries and allow us to gaze voyeuristically at other people's lives, I would question the cliché that travel broadens the horizons. What horizons?

Jim and his dog were always up and down Sandy Lane, which skirted the edge of the golf course. We'd often see him when we drove our mowers and tractors up and down the lane, in between the old barn that was our machine shed and the various entrances to the golf course. Jim had somehow trained his dog to hunt out golf balls, and he made a few bob selling them back to golfers. He was amused by golfers. He considered them to be 'townies', and if some of them lived in the country, well, what was the country becoming anyway but an extended suburb of the town? Jim's amusement never seemed to contain resentment. Whatever life chucked at you, that's the way it was. Always had been.

Anyway, Jim knew that my surname was O'Leary, and to him this meant that I was Irish. Oh, should I witter on here about stereotypes? I don't think so. That I should be knocking the dew off the grass in the morning caused him to go into paroxysms of wheezing laughter about leprechauns and the like. But the area had its own folklore, and now, I think, Jim is part of that folklore.

Jim never got used to the new ways. Agriculture changed dramatically during his lifetime as a farm worker, and insecticides and herbicides became a regular part of farming. When Jim had been out spraying, with his backpack and no protective gear (which, even if it had been used by the average farm worker in those days, he would have looked down on as being a bit namby-pamby) and the nozzles had become blocked, he would put the nozzle in his mouth and blow on it, in order to clear the blockage. This was a very bad idea – the insecticide and herbicide got into his lower lip and rotted it away. Jim had to go to the hospital in Winchester, which was an epic journey for him, and have the remains of his lower lip cut off, the skin then being pulled up over the gums (he didn't have any lower teeth) to make a substitute lip.

Jim used to wear a big hat, he had big, bushy eyebrows and he always had a pipe clasped between his upper lip and his lower non-lip, through which he smoked a very strong tobacco. You could tell when Jim was coming down the lane, because you could smell his baccy smoke. My mate Victor, who still lives near Sandy Lane, says that sometimes he can smell Jim's baccy smoke even now, when he's taking the dog out in the evening. He's probably pulling my leg, but I can still feel Jim's presence in old Sandy Lane.

Anyway, one night in the early 1970s, Jim and I went for a few pints down the Wheatsheath.

It was nearly midnight when we wandered up Sandy Lane and stopped by the gate to the old orchard. I always used to climb over this gate to get back to the caravan where I lived – I'd then thread my way through the orchard, go round Basil Gamblin's pond (a dreary old place all surrounded by elder bushes), across a couple of fields, and back to the caravan.

Anyway, I piddled on the left-hand gatepost, whilst Jim piddled on the right-hand gatepost, then we leaned on the gate and carried on talking. I loved listening to Jim talk about how things used to be in the Hampshire countryside, and it certainly wasn't all rosy, romantic stuff; he'd had a hard life. I'd think about all the changes that had taken place during the twentieth century, and Jim's life throughout this; one that was at the same time insular, and intensely adaptive.

'Have you heard tell of wassailing the orchard?' asked Jim. I hadn't. I remembered the carol, 'Here we come a wassail-ing', but that was about it.

'Years ago,' said Jim, 'on twelfth night – that's twelve nights after Christmas, the old New Year – we used to get in the orchard and make a big noise. We'd fire our shotguns up in the air, we'd ring bells, we'd bang pots and pans together, and we'd sing special wassail songs, and shout wassail shouts.'

I was interested in this. In my experience people didn't talk so much about old traditions; it was more something that you read about in books.

'Then we'd get some cider and we'd pour it around the roots of the big tree in the middle of the orchard, that's the one we used to call the Apple Tree Man.'

'What was all that in aid of?'

'To drive out the evil spirits, to make sure that when autumn came there'd be big juicy apples on the trees – to bring good luck to the orchard.'

'I don't suppose anyone does it anymore,' I said,

implicitly inviting Jim to make some comment about modern carelessness.

'Well, if they was, they'd be doing it now, seeing as how it's Twelfth Night.'

My ignorance of that made me the example of modern carelessness, there never was any point trying to pander to Jim's prejudices.

'No one's wassailed the orchard since the 1920s,' continued Jim, 'a lot of the men never came back from the first war, and the custom died out. So listen, nipper,' – Jim called everyone younger than himself 'nipper', and given that he was ninety-six that was everyone, except for Mr Baker, who was a hundred and three and lived down in Wickham – 'whatever you do tonight, don't take a shortcut through the orchard, cos you'll upset the Apple Tree Man. No one's wassailed him for years, so he'll be firky like; he'll won't like folk.'

Now, I thought that Jim was joking – he was like that – he'd say something completely daft, often playing up to what he considered to be a townie's stereotype of a country man, and keep a completely straight face.

'Yeah, all right Jim,' I said, 'but you know that's my shortcut home.'

'I'm not joking, nipper, you'll upset the Apple Tree Man.'

'Yeah, yeah,' I said, looking for the sparkle in his eye.

He erupted. 'You nippers, you thinks you knows it all. Well, go on, go and find out for yourself!' And off he went – humpety hump – down the lane.

Oh Lord, I didn't want to upset him. If I'd thought that he was serious, I would have taken the long way round, but he'd gone now, so I thought I couldn't upset him any more than I had already; I might as well take the shortcut.

So I did.

I climbed over the gate and started to walk through the orchard.

It was a neglected orchard; no one looked after it anymore, no one thinned out the branches, which were all twisty, tangled, and gnarly. There was a bit of a breeze kicking up, and the trees were creaking and groaning in the breeze. I felt that I was an alien, unwelcome visitor amidst complaining trees, and started to wish that I'd taken the long way round.

Then I reached the big tree in the middle of the orchard, the Apple Tree Man. Apple trees are twisty and gnarly anyway, but this one was exceptionally so – and the whorls and knots on its trunk looked like ancient faces, faces with no great friendly intent.

'Don't be stupid,' I said to myself, 'just keep walking.'

And then I had that feeling: the feeling that there was someone – or something – behind me, looking at me. I can't describe the feeling; I'd better leave that to Coleridge:

> Like one, that on a lonesome road
> Doth walk in fear and dread,
> And having once turned round walks on,
> And turns no more his head;
> Because he knows, a frightful fiend
> Doth close behind him tread.

… but I did turn my head again, because I felt a clap on my shoulder, and there, in the murky darkness, was a hand. Or was it the branch of a tree? I looked round and found myself staring straight into the face of the Apple Tree Man.

There was a weight on my head, and a weight on my body. I was lying down.

The cold from the ground was spreading into my body, into my bones. My limbs were heavy – like one of those dreams

where you know you're dreaming, but you can't wake up, as if there's something sitting on you and holding you down.

Like being hag-ridden.

And the Apple Tree Man was in my head – pips and twigs and seeds and sap and roots and trunk and branches and dry winter leaves.

And I saw Sandy Lane, twisting its way down the edge of something – the world? – like a snake.

… And there was a settlement, at the sharpest bend in the lane, where the archaeologists found the Mesolithic arrowheads, watched by Jim Privett, bemused by these daft townies, who dug into the ground with silly little trowels, and washed elf stones. But I saw the settlement, with smoke trailing up to the sky, and the old ones knapping flints that had been brought in from elsewhere.

… and the lane kept on sinking into the ground, and shacks and hovels came and went by its deepening sides, and I tried to get up, or wake up, and I couldn't fight my way out of it.

… and the Waltham Blacks walked furtively down the lane. Poachers, their faces blackened with charcoal and gunpowder, walking towards the death of a gamekeeper and the drop at Tyburn.

… and all those deaths that the lane led to … Peter Cluer of Clewer's Hill and a chaotic fight, lonely suicides, the natural passing of lives; but lives so often shortened by their harshness.

… and death himself, with his rags and his scythe, clattering down the lane in an ancient cart pulled by a skeletal horse, piling up the cart with corpses.

… and the red eyes of death, staring out from under a raggedy hood, looking like the eyes of an albino badger – the badger that was dug up, baited, and clubbed to death, during the time that I lived there – and the bodies of his tormentors where piled on the cart.

… and then there where the adulterous couples from Gosport and Fareham, who had found this secluded spot, and suffered the most terrible coitus interruptus when they'd seen Jim's distorted face peering through the car window, a cloud of smoke emanating from the greasy old pipe clasped between his gums.

… and then the tree was a leper, who had abandoned the 'pest house', and was alone, at the edge of the world.

'Get up,' said the leper.

But I couldn't, for I was younger than the date, and a computer programmer lived in Jim's house, and a whole network of shimmering branches, roots, fairy rings: mycelium fizzled and crackled through and around Sandy Lane – and golfers were knocking balls about on both sides of the lane, and the land was dotted with livid green patches awash with nitrogen.

'What's to come?' I managed to ask, my mouth full of cold and soil and frost.

'Find out for yourself, I have my own problems, but this lane is mine.'

I think I got up then, but I'm not clear about that. I think I stumbled past Basil Gamblin's Pond – and for all I know the black cats were a'flying around on broomsticks – and somehow I was in my bed when I woke up halfway through the next day, covered in scratches and bruises.

It was a few days later that I saw Jim. I was walking down the lane with Victor – both of us carrying our switching rods ready to spend an hour knocking the dew off the grass. Jim was leaning on a gatepost, puffing on his pipe.

'I met the Apple Tree Man,' I said.

Jim gave me a pitying look.

'I did, I fell on the ground and couldn't get up.'

'Can't take your drink, nipper,' said Jim.

Victor laughed. 'Lightweight,' he said.

'They're all bloody mad round here,' I thought, certain of my own sanity, and started looking forward to a good slice of lardy cake.

4

THE ANDOVER PIG

Why is it that when someone chooses to believe in reincarnation, and then, further, believes that it is possible, somehow, to trace their former incarnations; those incarnations turn out to be ones that flatter the, possibly rather dull, current incarnation. It has to be Cleopatra, or Genghis Khan, or Queen Elizabeth I, or else a supposedly romantic villain like Dick Turpin, or a tragic figure like Anne Boleyn. Why is it never Edna or Fred, who never did nuffink much, or Ug, who was a bit further down the evolutionary ladder, and sadly perished when he fell into a bog whilst searching for tasty grubs?

Then again, if life is a force, or energy, or a spiritual whirligig – something that constantly spins around us like berries in a blender – why does the past incarnation have to be another human being? Why can't it be a blob fish, or a spider, or a parasitic flatworm, or a dandelion, or a pig?

It's the same with ghosts. I suppose ghosts aren't always the shades of people – they can be demons or some such – but if the ghost is the ghost of a formerly living being, then it tends to be the ghost of a human being.

Except in Andover.

In Andover there is the ghost of a pig, but it will only manifest itself during a violent thunderstorm. Now this ghost is

mentioned in that wonderful WI publication *It Happened in Hampshire*, but I first heard about it at an Andover festival.

I do get to tell stories at some strange events, and this was an event for bikers. I was telling stories to bikers' children, rather than the bikers themselves, though they were, to be fair, an amiable bunch – whilst sober anyway.

The festival was run by a local butcher – a highly motivated biker butcher – and it was called the Hogroast Festival. It centred on the spit-roasting of several pigs and the smell of crackling and cider is, to me, an aroma that should be bottled so that I can spray it under my armpits. I loathe the mass production and intensive factory farming of animals, so I have no wish to offend vegetarians, whose stance I respect, but pork crackling is, to me, bliss.

I was admiring a Screaming Eagle motorcycle, belonging to a local road rat, being particularly impressed by the bottle opener that was built into the side panel. The owner was doing that thing that I can really find rather irritating

– 'You think *you* know about stories, well let *me* tell you a few things …' – which I often get from taxi drivers and aged folk singers, so when he started on about a ghostly pig that manifested itself over Andover during thunderstorms, I naturally assumed that he was taking the piss.

But later on I read about it in the WI publication, and then was also told that there was a mention of it in Karen Maitland's *The Vanishing Witch*, so I looked into it further.

Who was it who revealed the whole story to me? I think it was that woman who must have been a reincarnation of Old Nan, the wise woman, who used to live in a rickety-rackety wooden hut on the edge of Harewood Forest, close to the banks of the River Test, a place not so far from Andover.

It was in Harewood Forest that King Edgar the Peaceful (who was far from peaceful) took the opportunity of a wild boar hunt to run his friend Ethelwold through with a spear, because he wanted to steal Ethelwold's wife, Elfrida. However, if you want to know that story you'll have to read *Hampshire and Isle of Wight Folk Tales* by that renowned historian Michael O'Leary. It was after Edgar's marriage to Elfrida that the events of our story take place.

Now, when a hunter chased the boar, he wasn't embarking on an easy quest. Wild boars are formidable quarry, and can turn on the hunter with lethal tusks and teeth, all backed up by massive weight and force. When a fox hunter dons the funny clothes and, cutting a dashing figure, gallops across the fields in pursuit of Reynard, it is unlikely that the fox will turn round and savage the hunter. The wild boar, however, now that's something else.

Edgar had been pursuing a particularly fearsome boar through the depths of Harewood Forest, and the weather changed during the hunt. The air became prickly and charged with static, and the sky grew darker with the distant rumbling of thunder. Now, when hunting the boar the hunter doesn't rely on hounds to do the dirty business for him, he has to position himself, dismount, and face the beast whilst brandishing his boar spear. Usually there will be several hunters doing this, but Edgar found himself separated from the others and, as he valued his reputation for being a proper, macho sort of a king, he thought that he'd face the mighty boar alone.

When the enraged boar, it's great jaws foam-flecked, came thundering out of the trees, it was brought down by a lunge that was both lucky and skilful. The spear was thrust deep down the boar's throat and the great beast lay twitching and shuddering on the forest floor. Edgar drew his horn ready to summon the others, but then there was a flash of lightning, an almighty rumble of thunder, and a shuffling and grunting sound, followed by an overwhelming stench. A wild boar has a strong smell, of course, and this contained elements of boar musk, but the overwhelming sense of it was the sweet, rotting stench of death.

Edgar readied himself for another attack, but without his former sense of confidence. This time he felt a fear that threatened to engulf him; the sound of the creature, grunting and shuffling, was more like the sound of human feet than the passage of a wild boar. The sound turned and started to move away, and Edgar followed the clear track that it left behind.

He entered a clearing, and in the clearing was the hut and kiln of a charcoal burner.

Charcoal burners – those solitaries of the forest who live out their lives in the deep, dark woods. The other people. Those around whom people skirted – both contemptuous and afraid.

The king strode into the clearing. The charcoal burner, seeing the royal figure, fell to his knees and muttered. The wind whipped up and there was another clap of thunder.

'Where is it?' roared the king.

'Where – where is what, My Lord?'

'The boar, you fool, where is it?'

''Tis no boar, My Lord, 'tis mine.'

'I'll have your head,' bellowed the king, and, ignoring the kneeling charcoal burner, he strode up to the hut. The first drops of rain came whirling down through the wind as the king hammered on the door. There was a shuffling and grunting from inside, but no sign of the door opening. So, as a vivid streak of lightning forked across the sky and the rain tore down, the king kicked the door open.

What lurched out wasn't a boar, though it had a boar's head. It had two legs, and a rotting body comprised of a terrible mixture of body pieces. It grasped the king's head in great calloused hands and, as a bolt of lightning struck the charcoal kiln, twisted it and tore it off.

The creature shuffled back into the hut, followed by the charcoal burner, and snuffled around a little bit. The smoke-blackened, wrinkled charcoal burner looked down at the creature as it moved around the hut. It was little more than a bag of flesh and bones; bits of body fixed together – bits of this, that and the other. Higgledy-piggledy-wiggledy. A brain animated by a spark of fire from a charcoal kiln; or fluxed into awareness and motion by an organism usually associated with rot and decay; or convulsed by lightning, the body jerked into a semblance of life.

A creature made from the bones of unwary travellers, mixed with the remains of the inbred foresters and charcoal burners who had died deep in the forest and remained unburied, with no funerary words said over the corpses. And the creatures of the forest: the great boar, the brown bear, old Brock the badger.

The charcoal burner dragged the body of the king by its legs into the hut and set to work.

The thing that finally arrived back at the king's hunting lodge was a parody of the king; surely taller, with a terrible smell. But then the king was pretty much a parody of himself anyway – a loudmouthed swaggering braggart. Possibly, Queen Elfrida, back at the court in Winchester, wouldn't be so much more disgusted by this composite of corpses entering her bed, than by the real king; but she was saved any unpleasantness, because he died that night, choking on a fish bone. They were quick to shove him in his coffin, where the mixture of vapours caused the body to explode before burial.

As for the queen, the next in line to the throne was Edward, Edgar's first son before his marriage to Elfrida, so she travelled down to Corfe Castle in Dorset and murdered him, thus ensuring that her son Ethelred should become king, though he wasn't really ready.

Long after that time the modern town of Andover appeared; a town oddly disassociated from its surroundings, as if parts of a larger city had been plonked down into the countryside. The town has swallowed up the area of the haunting, but the haunting continues, and why not? During a thunderstorm a crackling, luminous, levitating, ghostly pig is said to appear, and then disappear with the next flash of lightning. Many residents of Andover claim to have seen it, especially, for some reason, since the 1960s. In the 1930s the ladies of the WI, in *It Happened in Hampshire*, wrote that it first appeared during a thunderstorm, and is only seen on New Year's Eve, but maybe it's grown more active since then. I wouldn't know, people always recount stories differently.

More scary, I think, is the other ghost, or possibly something still living, or half alive, that is sometimes heard grunting or snuffling in nearby Harewood Forest. Best not go there at night.

So now, if I find myself at a hog roast, gazing at the pig rotating on a spit, I tend to feel that this is an undignified way for a beast to end its days. Maybe if we'd faced the danger and excitement of the hunt it would be different. The animal, however, hadn't been factory farmed, the biker butcher was conscientious with his sourcing, and it wasn't being presented to us as fragments wrapped in cellophane, leaving the consumer unaware of its sentient origin. However, if all the animals we used and killed came back to haunt us – then there really would be no rest for the wicked.

5

BURNT HOUSE LANE

Burnt House Lane in Bransgore isn't the only lane in the country with that singular name – there are two more in Hampshire and a couple on the Isle of Wight, let alone all the others throughout England. People who live next to, or near, one of England's Burnt House Lanes will have their own explanation for the name, and, being unaware that there are so many other Burnt House Lanes, will be certain that their own personal explanation is correct. Often this is the story of a house fire and a sad death, sometimes a murder and an arson, and not infrequently, a haunting.

I wonder, though, if the ubiquity of the name is due to the past presence of brick kilns; certainly I know that quite a few of them did have brick kilns next to the lane.

At one time England was dotted with brick kilns – strange conical chimneys where bricks made from the local clay were fired, something that, strangely, was brought home to me in airspace above India. I remember the time I was flying into Amritsar, in the Indian Punjab, and as I peered out of the window of the Turkmenistan Airways jet, as it bumpily circled the old city, I was looking for a glimpse of the Golden Temple. I was struck by a feeling of déjà vu, which had nothing to do with the temple, but something to do with scores of strangely shaped buildings emitting plumes of smoke.

'What are those?' I asked my Punjabi companions.

'Brick kilns.'

Well – of course – these were buildings so ubiquitous they were hardly worth noticing. But I couldn't work out why I felt such a sense of déjà vu – until, that is, I remembered a painting displayed in Southampton Art Gallery – a painting that took as its viewpoint an imagined aerial position – a picture of a rapidly expanding Southampton painted by Phillip Brannon in 1856 – and it is dotted with brick kilns, just like Amritsar was as I looked out of the plane window.

Anyhow, Burnt House Lane in Bransgore used to have a brick kiln, and in *It Happened in Hampshire* Beddington and Christy wrote, in 1936, of a little boy who used to be seen running up the road, 'crying bitterly, but never allowing himself to be touched. He always disappeared in some bushes in the pool of a disused brickyard, near where, it is said, a wicked couple lived who drowned their children because they could not afford to keep them!'

Ah – the wicked couple.

But then Bransgore, and particularly adjoining Thorney Hill, was a place for the marginalised – it was also well known as the home of New Forest Gypsies – and brick kiln workers, like charcoal burners, had always had a touch of the 'other' about them; they still do in India. If the boy had drowned in the pond, in a ghastly accident, isn't it easy to imagine the suspicions of the more comfortably off, suspicions partly motivated by an unconscious feeling of guilt, blaming the parents and compounding their misery.

And he's not the only child haunting Burnt House Lane. There's the little Gipsy girl, who suffered terrible burns when her pinny caught fire. Alice Gillington wrote about her. Gillington was an early twentieth-century collector of Gypsy songs and folklore, and also a writer of the kind of story poems popular at the time, and her description of the girl's death, in a *Country Life* article, is rather shocking in its unexpected lack of sentimentality – with its prosaic details – the baby not letting go in time, the girl's sister never having the chance to say goodbye:

As we went our way up the road, Lily was telling me about her little sister, Rosy, who was burned to death last year. It all happened so suddenly; there was no time to help her. The mother was out with her flower baskets and the children were at play at home. Rosy was making 'fags' out of pieces of paper, 'to smoke' the child said. All at once, as she was holding her papers at the fire, a bit of one of them got ablaze and dropped onto her pinny. Lily had the baby in her arms at the moment, and the baby wouldn't let go so that she could undo Rosy's pinafore in time. Rosy had screamed that the fire was going to her head, and rushed out into the garden. A neighbour, hearing the screams, ran out to the child, wouldn't let her indoors for fear her whole cottage would catch alight, but laid her down on the stone doorstep and threw a sack over her. But that didn't put the fire out. Then she threw something else over her and at last quenched the blaze. But the fire had done its work; and when the father came home from his labour and the mother from her flower-hawking, nothing could be done for Rosy. She was terribly burnt and died shortly after, in hospital.

'Did you say good-bye to her?'

'No I didn't. They took her away d'rectly mother came 'ome, and I never saw her no more.'

And then – there's an adult ghost in the lane – but he's just a shade – 'a vapour thing' – that 'swiffles' across the road. Alice

Gillington wrote about him too, when describing the fear of a local woman:

> She was afraid to pass the sand-pit, that deep sand-pit fringed with firs, because of 'that there vapour thing,' that 'swiffled' across the road between the sand-pit and the Seven Firs. What the story was, no one knew, or no one cared to tell. Foresters never give you a direct answer if they can avoid it, especially to a stranger. Even in the simplest matters this particular caution and superstition shows itself in evasive looks and lying answers. The gipsies, on the contrary, will tell you straight that there has always been 'something to be seen' thereabouts. One or two of them have seen the man in black in the half-light of a winter's morning, when they were coming out of a by-lane with a holly cart.

I was fascinated by this anecdote, so I thought I'd ask Geoff about it, because Geoff knows a thing or two about the Forest.

I'd like to describe Geoff in a way that would depict him as a romantic denizen of the New Forest; to say that he was a New Forest commoner, or that he was a New Forest Romani, or that his ancestors had lived in the depths of the Forest for generations; but that just isn't the case. A lot of people who have wandered the Forest for years have no origin there – well, I suppose that I'm a prime example, living in inner-city Southampton since the 1970s yet constantly roaming the Forest – but always, in a strange sort of way, a tourist. Indeed, nowadays, like most of the people who live in the Forest.

Anyway, Geoff is a retired postman from Camberwell. He's a keen cyclist, and all his life he's cycled the Forest. Now, in retirement, he spends more time there than he does at home, frequently bivouacking out in the woods. Geoff is a practical man, and not one to go on about ghosts and stuff, but he's inhabited the Forest, him and his bike, in all seasons and all weathers, and all the old Forest people know and accept him.

Meeting Geoff one summer's evening in the garden of the Crown at Bransgore, I pressed him for any knowledge of the Burnt House Lane shade.

'It's whoever you want it to be,' he said enigmatically. 'Well you call yourself a storyteller, you should know, it's the one who tells the tale.'

'What are you on about? How much have you drunk that you have to go all woo woo on me?'

'I do know about that ghost, but you'll have to listen, and stop being a smart-arse.'

Where do I start the story?

Often Geoff just pushed his bike, sort of leaned on it, listening to the wheels click-click and just letting the motion of walking and pushing take him. It was evening, getting dark, and he was ambling down Burnt House Lane. There are a lot of houses along the lane now, though it still has a rural feel to it, and there are also areas of woodland and compounds full of bits and pieces, including a Southern Gas sub-station.

'There was a boy running, crying, and he was saying, "I never, I never",' said Geoff.

Geoff called out 'Wait' to the boy, though he immediately knew it was a ghost. He felt cold – suddenly cold – that cold in the bones that makes your heart flutter and shifts your bowels a bit – but it was a child, and it seemed to be a terrible injustice that a child should be a ghost – that a child should remain glued to the earth and locality.

'Wait,' Geoff called out again. 'What is it?'

'I never,' said the boy, and his face seemed white and featureless, and his eyes looked like dark, ragged holes.

'You never did what? Who said you did?'

The boy disappeared through a hedge into a hollow at the edge of the woods.

''S all right, Billy,' said the burnt girl, 'see, that man'll tell us a story.'

And then the hollow was full of children, and they were clamouring and shouting and asking for a story, and Geoff grabbed his bike and pedalled away up the lane as fast as he could – which wasn't as fast as a shade swiffling across the road – but Geoff didn't want to be that shade.

And no more do I – so I'll keep the story second-hand, and not investigate too closely. But I can't work out whether it's a sad story or whether earthly pain has been ended; whether the children are children, or whether ghosts are real, or whether Burnt House Lane is really haunted – but I know that the shade could be anyone.

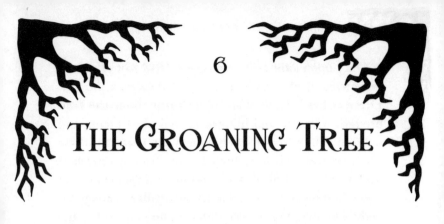

6

THE GROANING TREE

I 've heard the groan in the Forest. There are all sorts of things that can make a groaning sound – a deer barking, the limbs of a beech tree rubbing together in the wind, the sounds of nature red in tooth and claw; an owl swooping on a shrew, a fox snatching a rabbit, a weasel raiding a nest.

There is, however, a deeper groan, presumably something tree related because of the arboreal, 'woody' sound of it. The Forest doesn't always feel benign: sometimes unsettling feelings, thoughts and sounds seem to emanate from the tree line; and I've already mentioned Brian Vesey-Fitzgerald's comments about a feeling of hostility that he sometimes felt in the Forest.

The story that particularly describes the singular Forest groan is that of the Groaning Tree of South Baddesley.

Now this tree was an elm, and sadly we don't see many of them anymore; though some of the stark skeletons left over from the ravages of Dutch elm disease still stand in field corners. The elm tree has always been associated with death; maybe because they were once favoured as the tree from which to hang people, the elm is sometimes called 'the hanging tree', or maybe because coffins were made out of elm because it was good at resisting the effects of damp. But I'd better start the story at the beginning.

Once upon a time, to be precise a 1648 sort of a time, there lived, in the hamlet of South Baddesley, a cottager. Life was hard, Civil War raging throughout the land brought hardship and hunger, as well as suspicion and division. The cottager was getting on in years, for those times anyway, and scratching a living from his patch of land made for a difficult and precarious life. Sometimes, at night, he'd lie on his back and let out a groan. Though his body was exhausted, his sleep afforded him no rest because of the constant ache of hunger and his mind always being full of the worries of survival.

One night he lay in the darkness; he'd raked the ashes over the fire, and outside his cottage an owl called from a tree.

Suddenly there was a thunderous banging on the door.

Glory be – what was this? The cottager heaved his reluctant body out of his hard bed and stumbled to the door. He opened it, and there stood a tall man wearing a black cloak and hood – all that was visible of his shadowed face was the end of a long nose, pointing out into the moonlight.

The cottager's heart filled with dread at the sight of this apparition, and he knew by the quality of the cloak that this was a gentleman. The trouble was, you never knew if it was a Royalist gentleman or a Parliamentarian gentleman, and it always seemed that ordinary folk could find themselves dragged into trouble with no intention, and no escape.

'What is it, sir?' said the cottager, automatically touching his forelock.

The figure produced a note from his cloak.

'I want you to take this note to the king,' he croaked.

The king? What foolishness was this?

'The king, sir? How can …'

The figure produced a purse full of coins with the other hand, though it looked more like a claw than a hand.

'This is for you now, and there'll be more for you on your return.'

This was a fortune for the cottager; there was no question of refusal.

'But the king, sir …'

'The king is in Carisbrooke Castle. Give him the note.'

The cottager didn't have the first idea how he could give a note to the king, nor what all this could mean, but he had a purse full of coins, and the stranger told him to take the road to Lymington – so he hid the purse in a secret place up the chimney, and proceeded down the old sunken lane.

A short way down the holloway he stopped, glanced around, and started to tuck the note into the roots of a tree that was growing out of the bank.

'I said take the note to the king, you knave,' hissed a voice, and the terrified cottager looked round to see the tall hooded figure standing directly behind him.

'Yes sir, yes sir.'

This time he thought he'd do as he was told, and headed for Lymington.

It was early morning when he arrived, and – the strangest thing – looking over the reed beds towards the mouth of the Lymington river he saw no boats bobbing around, no people starting to move and get the fires going, no sign of life. He entered Lymington, and the town was eerily deserted, silent and empty. Down he went to a jetty and standing at the end of the jetty, wings outstretched, was a cormorant.

It looked at the cottager. The cottager looked at the cormorant.

'Get on my back,' said the cormorant.

'No,' said the cottager.

'GET ON MY BACK,' said the cormorant.

The cottager did so.

The cormorant then took a run down the jetty, and launched itself into the air, with the cottager sitting astride it, as though riding a flying horse.

'Which way is it to Carisbrooke?' squawked the cormorant over its shoulder, though I'm quite sure cormorants don't have shoulders. The cottager didn't know, he'd never seen a map in his life, and he'd certainly never flown before. The sea was beneath him, the chalk ridge of the Isle of Wight was ahead of him: but how was he to know where Carisbrooke was?

They flew into low-lying cloud and lost visibility.

'Which way is south?' croaked the cormorant. How was the cottager to know?

Then they dropped out of the cloud and the cottager could see blue water, a town, and a castle. The castle was a bit ramshackle, and there was a windmill built upon a mound – having never been to Carisbrooke the cottager wasn't to know it was the wrong castle. There was water, obviously the Solent, and there was a town, obviously Carisbrooke.

'There 'tis!' shouted the cottager, and the cormorant swooped down low across Southampton Water and into Southampton's rather ruinous castle. It deposited the cottager onto his bottom on a patch of grass, flew up again, and perched on one of the sails of the windmill.

To the cottager the approaching miller looked very important.

'Are you the king, your highness?' asked the cottager.

'Are you bloody mad?' replied the miller.

'I've a letter for the king,' said the cottager.

So the miller took the cottager to the colonel in charge of the Parliamentarian garrison at Southampton. The colonel had a look at the note, and things did not go well for the cottager. The letter was from Scottish Royalists who were plotting with the king (who was imprisoned in a rather open and liberal fashion in Carisbrooke Castle) to invade England. It was the discovery of this note that lead to the defeat of the Scots at the Battle of Preston, and sealed the fate of King Charles I. Not everyone knows that – neither does everyone know that after chopping Charles' head off, they stitched it back on again, so he'd look nice and tidy in his coffin.

As for the cottager – plainly it was the gallows for him.

Now, in Southampton, there was, until recently, a raised stretch of land near the docks, called The Platform. It had once been very important, a place where visiting dignitaries would parade up and down, where the local gentry would walk of an evening – and where the gallows used to be. I know of it because, when I was a council gardener, our mess hut was on The Platform. Southampton isn't a city that showcases its history; it is possible to visit and see nothing but retail outlets (that's what shops are called nowadays), but in this part of the old town there's masses of history: the old city walls, Gods House Tower, the oldest bowling green in the world, St Julian's almshouses in Winkle Street, the medieval Merchant's House, the Wool House, the Cloth Hall, Cuckoo Lane, Catchecold Tower, the Tudor House, St Michael's church, Town Quay – the list can go on. The Platform, however, seems to have slipped from notice, and during recent road development it was all torn away, leaving its only memory in the name of a nearby pub, the Platform Tavern.

So, in the 1640s, there was, on The Platform, a very fine gallows – and there had been much work for it in that turbulent decade. It was made out of elm, that wood that neither splits nor rots, the wood that carries the symbolism of mortality.

So: the noose was put around the cottager's neck and the hangman was ready to drop the trapdoor.

'Now's the time to say your last words,' growled the hangman.

The poor cottager looked down at the crowd – and amongst them he saw a tall black-clad figure, with a cloak and a hood, and the end of a long pointy nose sticking out of the shadow.

The cottager let out a terrible groan – a groan that told of the unfairness and helplessness of being caught up in the affairs of the powerful, a groan that told of the hardness and iniquities of his life, a groan that told of loss and humiliation; of horror and fear. As this desolate groan escaped his lips, the cords fell from his wrists, and the gallows started to vibrate. The executioner fell from the wooden platform, and the crowd screamed. The cottager clutched the gallows tree – and it took off, vertically, like a rocket. Up it flew, up into the clouds, where it levelled off, before it went into reverse thrust like a budget airline plane coming into Southampton International

Airport. It then descended into South Baddesley, and stuck itself into the ground behind the cottager's cottage. He staggered inside and flung himself onto the bed.

The next morning came, and the cottager woke up with the most terrible headache. He looked on the floor and saw the empty cider flagon.

'Oh my Lord,' he moaned, crawling out of bed and spitting into the fireplace. But then he felt up into that chimney cavity, and there it was – the purse full of money!

He stumbled out of the cottage, and looking behind it to where – surely – the gallows had embedded itself into the ground, there was an elm tree.

Well, after this the cottager prospered in a quiet sort of a way, and he lived a long life. He managed to keep his head down throughout the remaining shenanigans of the Civil War, and then through the Interregnum and the Restoration; continuing to simply live his life. Some put his quiet prosperity down to an involvement with smuggling out of the creeks and inlets between Lymington and Needs Ore Point, at the mouth of the Beaulieu river, but if that was the case, no one knew who he could be working with.

But what of the elm tree?

Well, this is the strangest thing. It always seemed to remain as a young vigorous tree, though around it other elm trees grew to stately height, passed away, and were replaced by yet more. This was remarked on only by the most local people, folk who counted the passing years in that little place, so the tree didn't draw any great attention until nearly a century after the events that I've just described.

It was then that the tree started to groan. This was not an average sort of a groan; this was a groan that was described in a pamphlet written in 1742 as a 'groan like a human creature in the agonies of death'. The pamphlet was entitled:

The Hampshire Wonder;
or The
Groaning Tree.
BEING
A full and true Account of the GROAN-
ING TREE, in the New Foreft, near
Limimgton in Hampshire.
WHICH Has been heard for fome Time paft by Thou-
Fands of People, who come from all Parts
To hear this amazing and portentous Noife.

This pamphlet went on to say that the groans 'are so terrible and shocking to human nature, that few who hear them have power to stir from the place till proper cordials have been administered to revive their sinking spirits and confounded imaginations'.

The pamphlet doesn't say whether the locals were managing to make a few pence selling the aforementioned cordials – possibly containing some smuggled spirits. It does, however, go on to further describe the groans:

They resemble in some manner the groans of a dying person, but withal so hollow and stupendously deep, that they seem to proceed from the inmost centre of the earth at least, and are so terrifying to the ear of human mortals, that it astonishes the very clergy themselves who have been to listen to it.

But then maybe the lives of people during the life of the tree had known much to groan about.

In 1750 a visit was made to the tree by Frederick, Prince of Wales. Oh what fun he and his courtiers were going to have. Edward King, in 1879, wrote, 'While there, the hoax of the

groaning tree was played off on the simple rustics, by some of the facetious courtiers who attended the Prince'.

Oh indeed? What happened next has been preserved in the oral lore of the Forest. One of the 'facetious courtiers' positioned himself behind the tree and commenced to groan. He soon stopped. The tree took up the groaning, but did so with such terrible desolation that the courtier must have attempted to flee. 'Attempted', however, is the operative word. In spite of a wide-ranging search, the courtier was never seen again. Some said that he was driven quite out of his wits, whatever wits he may have had, and became a feral mad man living in the depths of the Forest, like old King Nebuchadnezzar. Some said, however, that he never escaped the tree.

In an attempt to find out the cause of the groaning, a hole was bored in the trunk:

> Then in the trunk they bored a hole:
> This stopped the groaning evermore:
> For through the rift the imprisoned soul
> Flew out; it could not stand a bore.

So wrote Henry Doman, the Lymington poet, in 1867 (Doman is as fine a poet as Lymington's ever managed to produce).

After this the tree was uprooted. It was said that amidst the roots, petrified into elm wood, was the face of a human, a face contorted into a grimace of horror.

But maybe that's only a story.

7

BEWARE
CHALK PIT

There are rather a lot of headless horses in Hampshire – and not infrequently the rider, or the coachman of the carriage they are pulling, is also lacking a head – though sometimes they have the aforementioned head tucked underneath their arm.

At Copythorne in the New Forest we have an example of all of these; a coach driven by a headless coachman with his head under his arm, and pulled by headless horses. Further south in the Forest, Dame Alice Lisle, who was beheaded for harbouring fugitives from the Monmouth rebellion, is transported on dark nights from Moyles Court to Ellingham churchyard by a coach with no driver, pulled by headless horses.

The phenomenon still lives in the imaginations of children. Portsmouth is overlooked by a very singular-looking hill, Portsdown Hill, and when I've been storytelling in schools in Paulsgrove, Cosham and Hilsea, areas around Portsdown Hill, children have told me about the headless horse that gallops around the hill on wild and windy nights.

As far as I know, though, Farley Chamberlayne is the only place that has headless horses leaping through wormholes. It must be a wormhole, because it joins two distant places – and if it is highly fashionable nowadays to bring mentions of dark matter and other choice phrases pinched from quantum physics into narrative, well I can do it too! If I don't understand it, that makes me no different to anyone else.

Farley Chamberlayne is quite a remote place, and walking through the avenue of yew trees I've felt that I'm a long way inland; but, on reaching St John's church a view suddenly reveals itself; a view way over the Solent to the Isle of Wight, with the chalk ridge of the Island running the whole width of the distant horizon. Hampshire is hardly the Himalayas, but a hill is high only in relation to its surroundings, and Farley Chamberlayne is perched high and airy.

Inside the church there are wonders – a weathervane with a snake and an arrow has been brought inside, a mass dial – a sundial where you used to place your finger to show the time of the next mass – and depictions of some strange figures.

There is also a memorial plaque to one Thrift Smith. It reads:

SACRED
TO THE MEMORY OF *THRIFT,*
WIFE OF *JAMES SMITH,* FARLEY,
AND YOUNGEST DAUGHTER OF
JOHN HEDDERICK ESQ. PLEBHOLE
FIFESHIRE, NORTH BRITAIN,
WHO DEPARTED THIS LIFE
THE 2ND JANUARY, 1815,
AGED 27 YEARS.

Poor Thrift died in childbirth far from home, though she was loved and missed by her bereft husband. Plebhole, as written on the plaque, is Blebhole, sometimes known as Blebo, a small settlement not so far from Saint Andrews in Fife. In Blebhole there is a legend of a headless horseman, all dressed in black, who gallops fearsomely around Blebo Craigs and Kemback Woods. Thrift took the memory of her home way down south to distant Hampshire, and as she passed on, the spectres of home were drawn to her by her homesickness, as death made physical distance irrelevant.

The headless horseman leaps from his dark tunnel, passes St John's church, and gallops down the avenue of yews, before leaping again into the darkness that flings him back to Fife.

But if we can avoid wormholes to distant Scottish universes, and remain in Hampshire, let's further explore the area around Farley Chamberlayne.

Farley Chamberlayne sits at the edge of what is now a country park: Farley Mount Country Park. This is a glorious area of downland and woodland, centred round an extraordinary, pyramidal monument. The pyramid is hollow, and inside, on the north wall, there is a plaque with an inscription that reads:

Underneath lies buried a horse, the property of Paulet St John Esq., that in the month of September 1733 leaped into a chalk pit twenty-five feet deep a foxhunting with his master on his back and in October 1734 he won the Hunters Plate on Worthy Downs and was rode by his owner and was entered in the name of 'Beware Chalk Pit'.

This doesn't quite tell the whole story, at least not the way I heard it.

Yes, man and horse fell to the bottom of the pit, and the horse saved the man; and it's also true that the horse went on to win the Hunters Plate, whilst ridden by his owner – but the owner had changed.

When the horse fell to the bottom of the pit, he was lamed, and the great huntsman really wasn't so sentimental. The horse was no good to him now, so he allowed his groom, Joseph, to buy the horse at a knockdown price – something Joseph only did because he loved that horse.

The horse was able to carry Joseph, though he couldn't go beyond a walk, down to the pub at Hursley. One time Joseph had a few drinks, and got into talk about horses. Someone made fun of Joseph's horse and said he should be called 'Beware Chalk Pit', and – you know how it is, the beer flows, the tongue is loosened and impossibilities become possibilities – Joseph said his horse could beat any other horse hands down. 'Go on then.' Bets were taken, and Joseph was committed to the races that were to be held later that week on Worthy Downs.

As Joseph's horse ambled home, and as the cold breeze from the Solent started to blow up Joseph's nose, blasting the alcohol fumes out of his ears, he started to realise what he had done.

'Oh – poor old horse – oh what have I done? I just couldn't stand them lummoxes laughing at you. Poor old horse.'

Just then Joseph was startled to see a large white horse-head pass by. No body. No legs. No rider. Just a head.

'Good drop of beer the landlady keeps,' thought Joseph. Then a large white headless horse, ridden by a large headless rider wearing a scarlet hunting coat with enormous silver buttons at the back, drew level.

Joseph touched his forelock.

'Your honour seems to have lost his head,' he remarked.

'No I haven't, you bloody gurt fool,' said the head from underneath the rider's arm. It wasn't a pretty head; it had a mouth that went from one side to the other; sharp, pointy teeth; a skew-whiff broken nose; and two large, saucer-shaped eyes that shone like lanterns.

'Begging your pardon, your honour,' said Joseph, 'but as your head isn't on your body, I didn't know.'

'Well you should look before you opens your gurt, blubberin' mouth,' said the head from under the arm.

Joseph began to resent being spoken to in such a manner.

'Well, I'd think that any good Christian man should keep his head on his shoulders.'

'And I'd think any good Christian man wouldn't ride a lame horse,' said the head, at which words Joseph's nag broke out into a fine trot.

'Now, isn't that better?' said the head.

'Why, it is, sir, it is,' shouted Joseph, as the horse broke into a canter.

'So, Master Joseph,' bellowed the head, 'it'll be a race.'

'That it'll be sir, a fine steeplechase, and – and – Beware Chalk Pit is the finest horse in all the land.'

The phantom rider lifted up his head with both hands, stuck it fair and square on his shoulders, and whipped up his headless horse. Neck to neck, though not head to head, the two horses galloped down the avenue of yew trees below St John's church, as, with a whinnying like a thousand screams, the headless horseman of Blebo, time as irrelevant to him as distance, leaped from his writhing, squirming wormhole, and joined the steeplechase, all galloping headlong down the hill. As they leaped onto a moonbeam, they were joined by the headless coachman of Copythorne, and then Dame Alice Lisle herself, having taken the place of her non-existent coachman, was shouting on the headless horses of Moyle's Court, and then the headless horse of Portsdown Hill, followed closely by Hirondelle, the magical horse of Sir Bevois of Hampton, with the ghostly horses of Red Rice near Andover at the rear, but narrowing the gap.

With Joseph and the red-coated rider leading the pack, the steeplechase whooped down a moonbeam towards Tennyson Down (though it had yet to be given that name, because Tennyson was yet to be born) on the Isle of Wight.

And it's Joseph at the head, but no, the head is ahead, though the horse is behind; and it's Dame Alice galloping up on the inside, closely followed by the headless horse of Portsdown Hill, both of them passing the Copythorne Coach and the Red Rice riders. Hirondelle is dropping behind – that's what comes of having a French name; but Dame Alice can't pass Beware Chalk Pit; and they are thundering along Tennyson Down, to leap onto a moonbeam shining over The Needles, and into the final lap, up

*and over the farms and fields and rivers and streams and cities
and villages and woods and copses of Hampshire, and onto the
chalk ridge of Farley Mount, and as the hooves thunder onto the
turf, the head of the headless horse of the headless horseman is
just ahead of Beware Chalk Pit.*

The red-coated horseman stood up in his stirrups, lifted his
head high above his shoulders, and whooped, 'To me. Race
to me!'

'No, that's not right, your honorific,' shouted Joseph.
'Your horse's head was a head ahead of Beware Chalk Pit's
head; but if that head had been where it ought to have been,
then you'd have been a head behind.'

'Don't go losing your head over this, Master Joseph,'
said the rider, 'take him to the races at Worthy Downs,'
and then there was a scattering as the Copythorne coach
headed west, and Dame Alice headed south, and Hirondelle
headed east for Southampton, and the headless horse of
Portsdown Hill headed east for Portsmouth, and the Red
Rices headed north, and the headless horseman of Plebo
and his glistening black horse headed for their wormhole
and faraway Fife.

Well, Joseph rode home, sober as a judge now, albeit a
drunken judge. His wife didn't believe a word of his story
and gave him a wallop round the pate with the frying pan.

But Beware Chalk Pit was in tiptop condition, and when
Joseph took him to the races on Worthy Downs he came
in way ahead of any other horse, and given that he was a
complete outsider, anyone who had any money on him won
a fortune.

Maybe it was really one of those punters who built the
monument on Farley Mount, rather than Paulet St John esq.,
but the Farley Mount incident is remembered in a song that

I've heard in a few pubs over the years. I can't remember it all, but I remember the chorus:

> Beware Chalk Pit, Beware Chalk Pit,
> as you go galloping o'er the downs,
> Beware Chalk Pit.

8

GHOST ISLAND

There are areas of England that are particularly rich in archaeological discoveries – and you wonder what was special about those particular places. Then, if you look further, you will find that nearby there is a university with an archaeology department that specialises in whatever period is relevant – and they have carried out a lot of archaeological digs in their own locality. In other words, the cluster of discoveries is defined by the seeker, rather than by the distribution of sites.

It is the same with ghosts. The Isle of Wight has sometimes been called 'Ghost Island' because of all the recorded hauntings, but on closer inspection you will find that enterprising ghost hunters have sought them out, and set up tours and ghost walks – the relevant factor being the Island's status as a holiday destination.

I've written about the most famous of these in *Hampshire and Isle of Wight Folk Tales*, but of course there are plenty more. Personally, I'm not given to trailing around after the paranormal – it all gets a bit obsessive – and people do seem to be able to conjure up poltergeists when it might just as easily be a draught; or Grey Ladies at dusk, when shifting shadows so easily play tricks on the eyes. There are places, though, where I have felt that eerie feeling – and just wondered what is out there. One of those places is the long south-west coast of the Isle of Wight – the straightest stretch of coast on the Island's roughly diamond shape, with all those lonely beaches between St Catherine's Point and Freshwater Bay.

It's all very popular for windsurfing, kitesurfing, canoeing and the like – but it can be strangely bleak and eerie at night. One late evening I was taking a long walk up the coast, and ahead of me I saw a red light and a green light, like the port and starboard lights of a boat, but they seemed to be on the beach. I assumed I would catch up with them and find out what they were, but I couldn't. They were always the same distance ahead of me – it didn't matter whether I tried to run, or whether I stopped dead. I even wondered if they were lights on some sort of a buggy, but there were no tracks in the sand. I did feel spooked out; not in the grip of some terror, but odd, off kilter, shifted sideways.

But then strange lights seem to be a feature of the Isle of Wight. Wendy Boase, in her book *The Folklore of Hampshire and The Isle of Wight*, wrote about a doctor and his wife who saw the whole landscape lit up as if they'd entered a time-slip: 'The hedges and fields were a sea of luminous brightness. Across the road ahead of them were figures carrying flaming torches, but there was no sound and no colour except that of the lights themselves.' I do notice, though, that when such a scene is to be made believable, the person who recounts it must belong to a thoroughly respectable profession. Thus, the ghostly Grey Lady in the old hotel must be seen by an off-duty policeman, or the ghostly Roman soldiers that were seen crossing the road in Southampton must be described to us by a bank manager. If they are seen by a storyteller, or a professional ale taster, people tend to think that it's all made up. This in spite of recent revelations concerning the truth-telling capabilities of some of those 'respectable' professions.

Anyhow, on this long stretch of coast there would, at one time, have been plenty of smugglers' lights – and plenty of ghost stories to keep meddling people away when cargoes were being landed. There was also Atherfield Ledge, Brook Ledge, and Brighstone Ledge, all rocky outcrops that have, over the years, claimed ship after ship, and life after life. This has led to many reports of ghost ships, no doubt with their port and starboard lights a-twinkling, or disappearing down beneath the waves.

In 1839 Abraham Elder wrote about one of these, demonstrating in his book *Tales and Legends of the Isle of Wight* that he loved a good tale.

Elder tells us that along with his friend Mr Winterblossom and their guide, Ragged Jack the antiquary, they were talking to an old, blind corkhead. (Isle of Wighters of several generations standing are known as corkheads, or caulk heads – but for an explanation of that you'll have to read *Hampshire and Isle of Wight Folk Tales* by Ragged Jack's heir assumptive, Michael O'Leary.)

'I don't like talking about the ghost I saw,' said the old man.

'Did it look tall?' asked Abraham Elder.

'Very lofty, and she looked quite white like.'

Aha – a she. Questioned further the old man said he saw her 'some way out to sea, when I was smuggling in a boat. I have never been smuggling since, and never would again.'

'Could you see her legs at all?' asked Ragged Jack, who had heard the story before.

'Legs! No, what should she do with her legs, unless she were ashore?'

'Pray, what attitude was she in? What did she seem to be doing?' asked Elder, walking into a trap.

'She was in stays,' was the reply.

'Ah,' said Ragged Jack, developing a theme, 'I suppose some unfortunate creature that died of love and disappointment.'

'Dear, dear, dear,' said the blind man, 'I do not see how that could be. Whoever heard of a revenue cutter dying of love and disappointment?'

Well, Ragged Jack has had his fun, but then the old man tells his story. He tells how one evening, when he was young and he had his sight, and with the weather starting to kick up, he set off on a smuggling mission with two companions. Out at sea the storm really hit them. Showing no sail, and with their boat half full of water, they thought themselves lost. Then one of the men screamed out, 'We are run down!' and there was a great cutter, close-hauled, driving right on to them. 'Her bowsprit seemed to bury itself deep into the water, and a heavy sea tumbled into her, and then her bow tossed up into the air, so near that her bowsprit appeared to be right over us. We gave ourselves over entirely, when she suddenly luffed up.' She was tacking into the wind to avoid the smugglers' boat, and the men shouted, 'We are saved', assuming she would soon be on the other tack. But as her head turned into the wind, there was a terrible rattling of stays and sails – she couldn't complete the manoeuvre and was pushed backward by the tempest, her stern went under water, and down she went, stern first. The next sea rolled over her.

> Ah, sir, many a time before we wished them all [the excise men] drowned – many a curse we had heaped on them; but when their turn actually came, we felt for them just, if you will believe me sir, as if they had been our own children. Sir, they put down their helm just for the chance of saving our lives. Who would have expected that from men who earned their livelihood by hunting us down? They were fine fellows, though, that they were, though they sailed in a cutter.

But business is business, the weather cleared up, and the smugglers completed their journey to Cherbourg. They loaded their cargo, and with fine weather, they sailed for home.

Nearing home what should they see but the self-same revenue cutter, hove to before them:

> We could see the people on board just as plain as we ever saw anybody in our lives before. There was one man standing at the helm in a pea-jacket, and the skipper in a gold-laced cap, walking up and down the deck, looking as comfortable and as important as if he never had been drowned at all.

The skipper lifted a speaking trumpet and hailed them.

'Oh, such a dismal, hollow sound; it was more like the rolling of a distant clap of thunder than the voice of a living being; but then, sir, you must consider that the poor fellow must have been dead at that time somewhat more than six-and-thirty hours.'

The smugglers crowded on all sail and fled, all the time expecting a cannonball through their rigging, but there was nothing. When they looked back there was no cutter: 'In the spot where she was lying there was just a bit of mist.' Nearer to St Catherine's Point they saw the cutter again, a shadow in the rain that had set in, and in panic they cut away their tubs of smuggled spirits, and finally got home safely. They never went to sea again.

Now, what would the moral of that story be? Don't be considerate at sea? Trying to avoid collisions is a mistake? Drown smugglers, or you're liable to drown yourself? But then, what does a moral do to a story? It narrows it, takes away complexity and ambiguity; turns it into a sermon.

*

I don't know if there's a moral to the following story. It's a story that was told to me by a corkhead called Charlie, and he was certainly a man who liked a good tale. In some ways he expressed that through his leisure activity, which was being a Civil War re-enactor. I met him when I was telling stories at an event in Basingstoke, and he was quite a grizzled old bloke, one of the few re-enactors who looked like he really came from the seventeenth century. Charlie no longer lived on the Island, but he remained very fond of it, and to talk to him you'd hardly know he'd spent the last forty years living in Basingstoke. Sadly he died a couple of years ago; he had suggested that we write down his Isle of Wight stories, and like so many things, we never managed to get round to it until it was too late. I remember this one though, and if he was stretching the truth, or putting himself into a legend that he'd heard from someone else, well – don't blame me.

Charlie was a young man in the early 1960s, and one night he'd been for a pint or three at Freshwater and was pedalling back to the village of Brook in a wobbly fashion, down the Military Road, which follows the south-west coast of the Island; past Freshwater Cliff and Compton Bay, Shippard's Chine, Hanover Point and the fossil forest – with a big moon hanging in the sky and the sound of the sea. He wandered into the churchyard of St Mary the Virgin at Brook, in order to sit on a gravestone, roll up a cigarette and watch the stars and the glorious moon. Just then the church bell struck: 1, 2, 3, 4, 5, 6, 7, 8, 9, 10, 11, 12 – and a pause – 13.

Thirteen? Surely not. Then he looked up at the church and his befuddled brain took a certain amount of time to register that the church was different. It was older. St Mary's church is a fine Victorian building, built in 1864 to replace the old medieval church that burnt down in the previous year. Charlie was gazing at the old church. He looked round at the gravestones; they were decorated with pictures of mer-maids, anchors, ships in full sail, seashells and sea serpents. Then he heard the sound of the beating of a drum, and as he sat frozen on the gravestone, the figure of a mariner hove into view. At least it looked like a mariner, or a monster – or a drowned mariner. It was beating the drum, it had on the clothes of an eighteenth-century sailor, it was all festooned with seaweed and sea wrack, there were limpet shells on its skin, and its eyes shone in the darkness like pale yellow lanterns.

Behind this apparition there appeared two more, and they were carrying between them something sagging and drip-ping water, something wrapped in sailcloth.

Then, behind them, there was a drowned mariner playing a mournful tune on a squeezy box, and behind him a pale woman who moved slowly and gracefully, as if her body was animated by the movement of the sea.

The first mariner started to speak, in a voice from both close by and far away: 'We commit this body to the deep, to be turned into corruption, looking for the resurrection of the body, when the Sea shall give up her dead …'

Then they lowered the body into a grave that was adorned with a headstone decorated with a carving of a mermaid.

The woman offered her pale hand to Charlie, who sat like a stone carving himself, frozen with terror.

> Come take my hand,
> We'll leave the land,
> Come down with me,
> To the wine, dark sea.
> Come down the Chine,
> Forever mine.

Finally a noise seemed to issue forth from Charlie's throat; he said it was as if he was somewhere else hearing himself scream, and as he ran from the graveyard, the church became

its Victorian self. He fell over his bicycle, hauled himself back on to it, and pedalled off down the road as if all the demons in hell were following him – which maybe they were.

Well that's the story that Charlie told me, and you can believe it or not, as you please. Personally I'm glad that my only spooky Isle of Wight encounter involved nothing more than two lights. As traumatic as it must have been to Charlie, I'm sure, though, that it wasn't bad enough to be the reason for his move to Basingstoke.

9

CHUTE CAUSEWAY: STORY ROAD

In the north-west of Hampshire, near the borders with Wiltshire and Berkshire, the shape of the Downs is almost sensuous. Long, gentle curves, and from up on the slopes you can see the cloud shadows drift across the fields.

Up above Vernham Dean, on the ridge of the hills, Chute Causeway doesn't quite fit the sensuous curves. This is strange, because most written descriptions say that it does. It is a Roman road, and the point the authors of these descriptions are making is that it is unusual in not being straight; that the topography has forced it to follow the curving hill. But the Romans have built straight roads over much more difficult terrain than this. Should you walk it, should you look along it, you'll see that it is straight – it looks like a typical Roman road, but that every so often it bends – rather suddenly. Maybe this is to accommodate the shape of the hill, or maybe it is to avoid something. Walk it and you will see tumuli in the fields beside it, sometimes called Giant's Graves, and there are thickets, dense copses and quickset hedges. It goes around Haydown Hill, and it is high, light and airy – and yet, paradoxically, it also has a sense of darkness.

It is a storied road. I have described in *Hampshire and Isle of Wight Folk Tales* how the ghost of the rector of Vernham Dean toils up the hill to bring food and drink to the miserable plague camp he set up there – and how Mistress Plague herself can be seen careering along the thoroughfare in her black coach. The stories are not cheerful – they are dark – they are concerned with death and putrefaction, betrayal and guilt. There is also a sense of marginality about them, something which suits both the road's remoteness and its marking of the border between Hampshire and Wiltshire. The Romans must have had little shrines to their wayside gods at the bends in the road. With bountiful Haydown Hill so close, one might have thought they would have had a shrine to Ceres, or Demeter, the goddess of the harvest, but that seems much too cheerful for this brooding place, and in Roman times the hill was probably covered in dark forest – 'Chute' does, after all, mean forest. Perhaps, then, there was a shrine to Pluto, or Hades, god of the underworld, the Roman relation to all those deities and ancient kings sleeping under the hills of England.

Be that as it may, in the eighteenth century the road was considered to possess a very strange characteristic – it was longer one way than it was the other! Going east to west, you could walk it in twenty minutes, but perambulating west to east could take you all day. Some people would even walk all the way around Haydown Hill, down to Vernham Dean, and back up again, to avoid this. Little Persephone Goater (oh, the glorious names people had – look at those eighteenth-century gravestones and see names like Fortune Coker, Charity Singleton, Nathaniel Stone), well she was in service to the gentry at the big house west of the causeway, and it was Mothering Sunday. On this day she was allowed to take home a cake that she had baked for her mother – and Persephone's family, of course, lived east of the causeway.

As she headed down the causeway, clutching her precious cake, her shoes went *clip clop, clip clop*. They were good shoes, wooden shoes, solid shoes – and this was because her father was the best cobbler on the borderlands between Wiltshire and Hampshire. The phrase 'the cobbler's own children have no shoes' wasn't true in his case; he wasn't a man for fine words, but he expressed his feelings for his children by lavishing great care on their shoes; not so with his own shoes.

But, as little Persephone Goater trip-trapped along the causeway she felt that she was doing a lot of hard walking but making very little progress, a bit like walking the wrong way along a conveyer belt, though that may not be a very appropriate simile for the eighteenth century!

Taking forever to pass the Giant's Grave, she saw, at a bend in the road, a tall, dark figure.

'Whither away, pretty maiden?' asked the gentleman, who smiled with his mouth, but not his eyes.

Persephone felt a terrible dread envelop her, one that she had felt before when perambulating Chute Causeway 'the wrong way', but never this strongly, and there had never before been a gentleman standing in the road.

'I'm going home for Mothering Sunday,' said Persephone.

'And what do you have in your basket?' asked the gentleman.

'A cake for my mother.'

'Come with me,' said the gentleman, 'and I'll show you where you can pick flowers for your mother.'

'Oh no, sir, I've always been told not to leave the path.'

'I said, come with me,' said the gentleman, 'and you'll have all the cake in my kingdom.'

Now, Persephone's father was a practical cobbler, a man direct and to the point, and Persephone's mother was Tredeem Goater, known throughout the border country as a woman not to be messed with; so Persephone wasn't a girl so easily beguiled by a gentleman, especially one with cold eyes.

'No sir,' she said, 'I need to get on home to my brothers and sisters.'

The gentleman's voice became hard and threatening, 'You'll be coming with me if I say so, young woman.'

Then he looked down at her shoes.

'Fine shoes, fine shoes,' he ruminated, looking down at his own dainty, Italian brocade shoes that should have been the most fashionable of footwear, but seemed all burnt away, and rather hoof shaped, '… would I had a new pair of shoes.'

'Let me past, sir,' said Persephone, 'and I'll send my father, and he'll make you some fine new shoes. He'll have to come and measure your feet.'

'No one touches my feet,' screeched the gentleman, 'least-ways not without shoes on.'

'He can measure a foot with a glance, sir,' said Persephone.

'Hurry up, girl; hurry away and fetch him to me, or it'll be the worse for you. I'll come down and fetch the damn lot of you.'

Well, Persephone hurried home, and the road didn't seem so long.

Her mother was delighted with the cake, but not so delighted with the story about the gentleman.

'I'll fetch him one,' she bellowed.

'No,' said her husband, 'I'll measure his feet, a job is a job, and shoes for a gentleman will bring us good money.'

'There'll be no good money where that came from,' said his wife, ''twill all be wicked money – and he'll be dragging thee to hell or Haydown Hill.'

But her husband would go – and he put on his good clogs, just to make a show, and *trip trap, trip trap, trip trapped* down Chute Causeway. He was going the right way, so it didn't take him long to get to the Giant's Grave.

'Who's that trip trapping down my causeway?' said the gentleman.

''Tis I, Father Goater,' said the cobbler.

'You're the middle sized one, I'll warrant,' said the gentleman.

'I'm the man of the house,' bridled the cobbler, who took offence at the thought of his fair Tredeem being seen as less than dainty.

'Well, I need new shoes, but you will not touch my feet, cobbler.'

The cobbler looked down at the gentleman's burnt shoes, and said, 'I think, sir, 'tis the blacksmith you're wanting.'

'Don't talk back to me, cobbler,' shouted the gentleman, 'take my measurements, and make me a fine pair of black shoes with wooden soles that will not wear out on Chute Causeway, and that I can wear when dancing a fine caper on Haydown Hill under the light of a full moon.'

'Yes sir, yes sir – I have the measurements.'

'Then come with me, and we can make the shoes in my domain.'

'Oh no, sir, I must go back to my cobbler's shop, because there I have all the tools, and all of the materials.'

'I can find you anything, come with me,' insisted the gentleman.

'No sir, if you really want the finest shoes, I need to make them in my workshop. My wife will bring them, I would not deceive you.'

'Make sure that you don't,' said the gentleman, in the most threatening of voices.

Well, back home, Tredeem told her husband not to trouble himself making the shoes – although he would have done so.

She gathered up a rolling pin, and a cast-iron frying pan, and up with her along the causeway.

'Who's that trip trap, bloody crash banging along my causeway?' said the gentleman, as Tredeem's broad girth, round, red face, and enormous clogs rounded the bend in the road.

''Tis I, Mother bloody Goater,' she roared, 'and will you say "Whither away, pretty bloody maiden" to me?'

'Give me my shoes,' said the gentleman, 'or I'll drag you to hell and Haydown Hill.'

'Oh will you, my fine gentleman?' bellowed the largest of the Goaters. 'And I'll give you a gurt whack round the pate, and a clog up the fundament,' and she gave him such a crack round the side of the head with the cast-iron frying pan, that he spun sideways like a Catherine Wheel, and ended up back on his feet, with his head ringing like a bell. This was just in time to receive the clog up the fundament.

'Get thee back to bloody hell and Haydown Hill,' thundered Tredeem Goater, 'and you'll not be taking Persephone with you – and thank your bloody stars you haven't got me there, because I'd give you such a time that you'd wish yourself in heaven, as sure as heaven is your hell, and hell is your heaven.'

Well, the gentleman wasn't seen for a long time after that – but it's maybe that he's back on Chute Causeway now. People don't walk the causeway a lot nowadays, though it sees the occasional car hurtle along it far too fast. So, the gentleman may again be looking for souls to take under the hill, and if there's no one with the character of Tredeem Goater to gainsay him, he may well get his way. Just don't ever try to hitch a lift on Chute Causeway, because you may know the story about the vanishing hitchhiker, and it doesn't end well.

10

MARROWBONES HILL

When walking I can live in the present – it's when the worries and structure of my life disappear and I can just appreciate my surroundings; the different sound the wind makes in deciduous forest or coniferous forest, the patterns of sunlight through trees and the changes in temperature when the sun disappears behind clouds, the smells – the fresh smell after rain, or the smells of a dry, hot day. Of course consumer culture will even try to package this and sell it to us as 'mindfulness training' or some such tripe, but there is really something ancient about putting one foot before the other, and being open to one's surroundings – something that can put the detritus of living into perspective.

Anyway, I was on a long walk in the New Forest. I'd gone all the way from Winding Stonard, across Shifters Bottom, to Milkham Bottom, through the woods of Ellingham to the Great Bottom, then turned south again, past the pillow mounds of Big Whitemoor Bottom until I reached the houses around Linford. It was evening as I passed a farm and I began to think that I needed to pitch my tent somewhere. I thought I'd walk along the ascending valley of Linwood Bottom, through the trees, and up to Marrowbones Hill. I'd camp out there, and then the next day I'd wander into the metropolis of Ringwood along squelchy Foulford Bottom. It was really just the name that made Marrowbones Hill my destination, but it did seem such a wonderful name, and at least it wasn't a bottom.

As I headed down the farm track and into the woods, I got the feeling that someone was watching me – I turned round and saw, standing outside the farmhouse, hands on hips, a figure. But it was just a little too distant, and a little bit too dark, for me to make out the features. I didn't like the feeling that I was being watched, but I carried on walking.

As I entered woodland I could see no one behind me, but I had the sense of being followed, and that responsiveness to my surroundings, that 'in the moment' feeling, was gone – all I felt was the presence of someone, or something, behind me.

I left the woodland and found myself heading up to Marrowbones Hill. Up on the hill, all now illuminated by the light of the moon, there was a great spreading oak, surrounded, in a perfect circle, by holly trees. The hollies looked for all the world like dancers who had been suddenly petrified, like in one of those folk stories where villagers are turned to stone or trees for dancing on the Sabbath. Some of the hollies were locked together in embrace, making it look like the dance had been somewhat bacchanalian. I entered the circle, and saw, within, a strange oblong shape of livid green moss – livid even in the moonlight – all surrounded by elder bushes. It looked softer than the rest of the ferny, brackeny heathland, so I thought, 'That'll do, I'll pitch my tent there.' I stepped into the oblong, but as soon as I did so, everything went freezing, freezing cold. It was late, there was a clear, cold sky, it was October so it *was* cold, but this was different, this was a cold that came from inside me, from in my bones – this was a cold that told me something was wrong. I stepped out of the oblong – and found myself caught in a beam of light.

'What are you doing?' said a man, invisible behind the glare of his flashlight. 'You aren't allowed to camp in the Forest.'

'What's it to you?' I replied, adopting a resentful and rather unconvincing bravado.

'Why should the Forest be damaged by people being irresponsible?' said the man, lowering his flashlight.

'Who's damaging the Forest?'

'Camping in it can cause damage.'

'I never said I was camping,' I said, rather disingenuously, 'and have you really followed me all the way up from Linford?'

'I have,' he said, 'but not for my benefit, for yours – I know Marrowbones Hill well enough.'

Well, now I was intrigued, and what with that, and the unnerving change of temperature within the strange oblong, I sensed a story.

'Look,' said the man, 'if you like you can come down to the farmhouse and pitch your tent in the front garden. Then you can use the bathroom and toilet when you need to.'

I was surprised by this show of hospitality that seemed to follow hostility, and I felt rather glad to get away from Marrowbones Hill, so I followed him back the way I'd already come.

We reached the farmhouse near Linford, a prosperous-looking place, and he invited me in for a cup of tea. I met his wife, who was very pleasant and hospitable, and we sat down and talked about the Forest for a while. His wife said that she was going to have a glass of wine before going to bed, so they opened a very nice bottle of red, and got out the cheese and biscuits. After she'd gone to bed, the farmer opened another bottle, and our conversation became rather more lucid.

It was actually after he'd opened the bottle of malt whisky that I asked him why he'd said that it was for my benefit that I shouldn't camp on Marrowbones Hill.

'Listen,' he said, 'I'm a businessman – I'm not some "oo arr farmer" with a pint of cider; I'm part of an agricultural conglomerate, we have board meetings in London. If my business associates knew that I believed in such things, they'd never take me seriously again – so if I tell you, you've got to promise never to tell anyone else.'

So I promised.

And that should be the end of the story.

Because I promised.

And if I was to put it into a book, to be available to the public – that would be terrible.

But then you should never tell a secret to a storyteller, because they go blah blah blah, and I'm sure none of his important business associates would bother reading a daft little ghost book.

So here goes:

'When I was a boy,' the farmer said, 'I lived on this farm; it's been in the family for generations. Everyone said to me, "Whatever you do, nipper, don't go and play up on Marrowbones Hill, because it's a bad place."

Well, that's a fatal thing to say to a child, it just makes you more curious; so I was always up there, poking around to see what I could find. That strange oblong shape of green moss was there in the 1950s, and one time I was poking around in it and found a bit of old stick. I scraped the soil off with my thumbs, and there were cut marks on the end. It was a whistle. I blew on it, and I had that feeling – you know – "like someone's walked across my grave". But I took it, like you would, and off with me down the hill. Now, as I came out of the Forest into Linford, I passed the cottage where Jack and Mary Bottlesford lived – it's where someone's garage is now, you'll have seen that the new houses have got garages that are as big as the old cottages. Well, old Jack, he'd worked on this farm all his life, and he was leaning on the gate, smoking his old pipe.

"What's that you've got there?" Jack said to me.

"Oh, it's nothing, only an old whistle."

"A what? Where did you get that? Not up on … Marrowbones Hill?"

"Yes."

"Listen nipper, if I were you I'd take it home, put it on the fire, and burn it. BURN IT – TILL THERE'S NOTHING LEFT BUT ASHES." He was shouting now.

"All right, all right."

So I took it home, but I didn't burn it, of course I didn't. I put it in my treasure box, an old Oxo cube tin that I kept all my best things in, and put it under the bed. Then I forgot all about it, until the time that I woke up at midnight. It was midsummer's night, and the window was wide open, and you could see the dark forest leading up to Marrowbones Hill, with a big, full moon up in the sky. I woke up, because I thought I heard something, almost in the back of my mind, but coming from the hill. A whistle. Or maybe it was the cry of a vixen, or the screech of an owl. But I reached under the bed, I didn't know why, got hold of the treasure box, and took out the whistle. I blew it out of the window. There came a reply from the hill. Again I don't know why, but I got out of bed, tiptoed out of the bedroom, shutting the door behind me ever so quiet, so I didn't wake my mum and dad, crept down the stairs, avoiding that creaky one in the middle, put my coat on over my pyjamas, pulled on my wellies, then off and out the front door. As I walked along the lane, towards Linford Bottom, the whistles got louder and louder, till they sounded more like screams than whistles, and I could almost see them, like shadows around me.

Well, I now know that when I went past Jack and Mary Bottlesford's house, Jack and Mary were lying in bed; Jack would have been snoring away, but Mary was awake.

"Yere, Jack, I heard something." She shook him awake.

"What you talking about, woman?"

"I heard footsteps."

"Don't be daft, who'd be walking past yere, this time of night?"

"Sounded like child's footsteps."

Then, from Marrowbones Hill, there came the sound of a distant whistle.

"Oh my Lord, Mary, I knows what it is."

Jack jumped out of bed, quicker than he'd done in years, pulled on his coat and wellies, and went off up the hill after me.

But by that time I'd got to the top of the hill. Well, I stepped into that weird oblong, that always felt like it was some kind of containing space, and everything went freezing cold; you know about that. But as I did so, a cloud drifted in front of the face of the moon, and everything went pitch black, pitch dark. I was crouched there, sort of frozen to the spot, and there was something dark – darker than the darkness itself – squelching, sliding, slithering towards me. Just then, the cloud drifted away from the face of the moon, and everything lit up; just as old Jack got up to the top of the hill.

"It's alright, nipper, it's alright," he called out, "I've got you now," and he picked me up and took me back down the hill, back to Mary. Well, even though it was a hot summer's night, Jack lit a fire in the grate, threw the whistle in, and burned it; burned it till there was nothing left but ashes.

"I told you, nipper," said Jack, "I told you not to go up there. How many times did I tell you?"

Well, you can imagine me, sitting there clutching my mug of cocoa.'

'Yes, but what was it? What is up there?' I said.

'All right, I'll tell you.'

And now this felt a bit like one of those Russian dolls – there were stories within stories within stories.

The farmer continued:

'Jack said to me: "It was in the time of my grandfather …"'

Now this was the 1950s, Jack was an old man, so the time of his grandfather was back in Victorian times.

"There was this old woman, and she lived up on Marrowbones Hill, like they say old Brusher Mills did, in some sort of a bivouac of branches and twigs. She'd gone half daft – doolally – and she used to walk round and round Marrowbones Hill babbling stuff like "I be the guardian of this hill". Well, folk said she was a witch, but the minister at Linford said, "Don't be superstitious, picking on a poor old woman".

Anyhow, she died, just of old age, natural causes, a hard life. But after she died, the villagers from Linford and Poulner went up there and burnt her old bivouac down. Strange how folk are, because Victorian times, if you look at generations, really isn't that long ago. Anyways, all these bits and pieces fell out of the bivvy, things made out of wood and brambles, figures and creatures and wotnot – and I suppose that whistle, though they never found that – you found it, all those years later.'

Well, there I was, sitting at the farmer's table, guzzling his whisky, and listening, not just to his story, but to him repeating Jack Bottleford's story, and suddenly I felt a sense of disappointment. You see, I think I'd agree with the minister; there's this old woman, living all alone with the elements, and maybe she has dementia – and the people are getting on at her, calling her a witch. It's picking on someone who's vulnerable; it's bullying.

'So that's it,' I said, 'that's the story – there was a wicked witch living up on Marrowbones Hill.'

'Yes, that's it,' said the farmer, 'the wicked witch of Marrowbones Hill. Would you like another glass of whisky?'

'Yes, please.'

But as I held out my glass to the proffered bottle, I knew there was more – sometimes you just know.

'All right,' said the farmer, 'there is a little bit more, but I never told anyone this, I never even told Jack and Mary Bottlesford, so if I tell you this, you'll really have to promise never to tell anyone else.'

But it's all right; I had my fingers crossed under the table. He went on:

'Remember I said I was at the top of the hill, in that oblong shape of moss, and that there was something dark coming towards me? Well – before the cloud cleared away from the moon, before Jack got up there, something else happened. Suddenly all the fear just slipped away from me, I wasn't frightened any more, and what had been dark was light, and I seemed to see inside the hill. There were people there, but they weren't people, they were the "other" people – and time was different, what might have been only a night time to them, could be a hundred years to us – and there was music coming from inside the hill – only I didn't really hear it with my ears, more with my mind. The nearest I can come to describing it is to say it was like flutes and harps and pipes. And I was going to step into the hill – and if I'd done so, I seriously believe I would have become another statistic, a missing child. But it was then that the cloud cleared from the moon, and old Jack got up to the top of the hill, and said, 'It's alright nipper, it's alright'. And don't get me wrong, I'm glad Jack went up there, because I've got a good life; I've got my family, and I've got the farm. But sometimes, I'm ploughing the field down below the hill, at the edge of the woods, and I think to myself, "What if? What if I had?"'

Well, there you are, that's the story that the farmer told me as I sat at his table knocking back his whisky – and I realised that this was a folk tale, a tale of the other land under the hill. But this wasn't the west of Ireland, or the highlands of Scotland – this was Marrowbones Hill, on the edge of the New Forest. And I tell you what – I never will pitch my tent there.

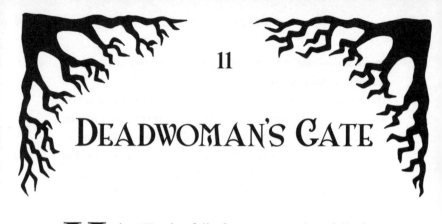

11

DEADWOMAN'S GATE

Hyden Wood is full of contrasts, and it's full of the physical evidence of its own history – fragments of buried stories. There can be a raised earth bank, and then suddenly, almost buried in the soil, there's a brick-built alcove, suggesting something of what went before, something built within the ground. There's humps and tummocks – evidence of something: a boundary? – a marker? – a habitation? – certainly a story.

And the contrasts? There most definitely are the 'deep, dark woods' – that alliterated phrase that makes a child listening to a story stop, and fearfully imagine, as they empathise with Little Red Riding Hood or Hansel and Gretel, being pixie led and lost in the forest.

But then the wanderer can emerge from the deep, dark woods suddenly into sunlight, and find a view that stretches across the southern slopes of the Downs to Portsdown Hill, then over the top of a hidden Portsmouth, to the cliffs of Bembridge on the Isle of Wight. Given that the Solent is as hidden as Portsmouth, those cliffs seem to be part of the mainland – and it is almost surreal to see tall cliffs in the gentle Hampshire landscape.

There is one part of Hyden Wood, though, where even on a still day a disturbing breeze seems to flutter and whisper, and where, even when the sun shines through the trees, creating dancing patterns of light, the air feels cold. It may be that in the evening you wander into the woods, with the warmth of a summer's day still hanging in the air; you might be feeling relaxed, pleasant, with the prospect of a summer evening pint ahead – but then you pass through Deadwoman's Gate. That's when the temperature drops, and that's when an oppression is liable to come and squat on top of your summery mood.

The stories say that a hand can burst out of the ground and grab your ankle, and should your feet stick in slummocky mud, you might well think, for a second, that the Dead Woman has got you. It is reputed to be a suicide grave – examples of which are dotted around Britain. Those folk who took their own lives, driven by a misery stronger than fear of any Biblical warning, and who were buried in lonely places, far from consecrated ground. There they are to be feared and ignored – so when it happens that a suicide grave, such as that of Kitty Jay on Dartmoor, mysteriously receives flowers, it is cheering to feel that the lonely and despairing, even after death, might get some degree of sympathy and recognition. These lonely graves are often at crossroads, and Deadwoman's Gate is just off the point where a forest track crosses what is now a tarmacked road.

It would seem that frequently the bodies that lie in these graves are the bodies of young women who became pregnant outside marriage, and their babies, whether born or unborn, have received no acknowledgement from the father. Young women faced with this stigma also faced the practical difficulties of being an unmarried mother, and the unwanted attentions of men who now put them into the smirking category of 'available'.

The story of Deadwoman's Gate, however, is a complicated and terrible variation on this theme. The suicide wasn't the unmarried mother, it was her grown-up daughter.

It was Saul the fiddler who fathered the daughter. In reality his name was Micheál, which to put an Irish name phonetically into English, is pronounced Me-Haul, but to English ears that sounded outlandish, so he became known as Saul, because it rhymed with 'Haul'. Saul was a peddler, but he also scraped out a rattling jig on the fiddle; that, plus his long, black curling hair, his easy charm, and his rather romantic outsider status, enabled him to cut a swathe through those inexperienced country girls, whilst all the while revelling in his own power. It was only one coupling that lead to the pregnancy, and Saul was gone – he ended his life older and weaker, the charm corroded away through a combination of alcohol and rough living after he'd taken up with one-legged old Fortune Dancey from Pewsey. It was she that pushed him into a Wiltshire ditch after a drunken argument, where he ended his life face down in his own vomit.

But as for the girl down in Hampshire, well she had given birth to a daughter, and she'd struggled through life. She looked after her child and herself as best she could, and she found that earning herself a reputation as a bit of a witch afforded her a certain amount of protection; and maybe some sort of respect borne out of fear. She knew her herbs and potions, she was better than most at applying them for healing purposes, and she could also make a curse sound menacing enough so that the very fear it induced could bring about its effects.

A landowner took a benign interest in the agricultural labourers thereabouts, and he gave her a small parcel of land in Hyden Wood. This wasn't of enormous value, but it was something, not least because various woodcrafts were important in the area, and so the daughter grew up amongst woodlanders, and when she came of age, she married a broomsquire from nearby World's End.

Broomsquires made besoms – broomsticks – usually made from hazel and birch. This was not an esoteric activity, besoms were (and still are) thoroughly practical sweeping brushes.

The daughter went to live with her husband in World's End, but they both cast their eyes on the little piece of woodland where the mother lived; it would be ideal for carrying out the broomsquire's trade. The mother, however, in her role as wise woman and hedge witch, wanted to keep her hovel on that land, and grow her own herbs and vegetables there.

The most poisonous of enmities are liable to come not between people who have always been enemies, but between those who were once close, and this mother and daughter must once have been as close as close could be, a little unit battling against the big, bad world. Their falling out, then, was terrible, and the bitterness between them was terrible. This wasn't something the broomsquire wanted, and he held no hatred in his heart for his mother-in-law, but, whilst he wasn't a bad man, he wasn't a strong one, except physically, and he did nothing to soften his wife's growing hatred of her mother, who she called 'that bloody old witch'.

And then came the bad winter; a winter coupled with an agricultural slump and the dreadful taxation required by a ruling class to fund its wars. The old woman (for she was nigh on forty) shivered in her hovel as a biting wind blew sleet in from the Channel, freezing the south-facing slopes of the Downs. It was only when she had no other choice that she went to her daughter and begged to be taken in. The broomsquire would have let her in, how could anyone do anything else? But the daughter gave her such a look – such hatred – estrangement – a look that echoed the expression the old woman could make when she pronounced a curse – and the broomsquire was too weak to intervene. The old woman stumbled back to her hovel, and that night she died of cold and hunger.

It was then that the realisation of the act hit the daughter; and her childhood, that close, intense, maybe claustrophobic relationship with her mother – the relationship that festered into hatred – rushed at her with the hopelessness and loneliness that her mother had felt when she was young and with child.

And so the daughter climbed the gate to her mother's parcel of land, at the crossroads in the middle of Hyden Wood, and hung herself from a beech tree.

As for the broomsquire, he was never the same again. He became a complete miser; after all, he had no one to share anything with. It was during one of his journeys around Hampshire selling besoms, mops and brushes, that he was murdered for his money. This was whilst he was staying at the Brushmaker's Arms in Upham, and it is said that his ghost still haunts the pub. Most accounts of Hampshire hauntings will mention it.

They don't, though, mention Deadwoman's Gate. Mind you, personally I'm not obsessed with ghosts, and as I've already said, I don't go chasing around after the so-called paranormal; I always go for the most prosaic explanation for unexplained events. But there is something about Deadwoman's Gate – something troubling, something disturbing – the flutter and sense of story and tragedy – the sense of the intensity of that relationship between the two women, the mother and the daughter. I would like to think that they could gain some resolution, even beyond the grave, and that the relationship could again be loving. Maybe it is – and maybe that's the problem. It could be that if, once again, it is the two of them against the big, bad world, and you or I pass through on that track through the woods, then we, the living, will represent to them that hateful, persecuting outside world, and we'd be better be very careful.

12

ONION'S CURSE

Calleva Atrebatum is a bit of an enigma. It is the remains of a Roman city at Silchester – a city that, when the Romans left, appears to have been completely abandoned. After a few hundred years the Saxons must have gazed on this crumbling, rotting city with awe. A place from a time more technologically advanced than theirs, with its hypocausts and latrines, its ceramic tiles and piped water. This is a science fiction concept, a futuristic city rotting before the eyes of the local people.

Why didn't the Saxons build on it? It does seem to be a feature of some Roman buildings that, maybe out of superstitious fear, the Saxons left them alone – but it's not always the case. The Roman fort at Portchester remained inhabited, as did Roman Winchester.

Perhaps there was something else at Calleva Atrebatum, something that caused it to be uninhabited to this day. There is something strange about the place.

A couple of years ago I was booked to tell stories in a village hall in nearby Tadley. Now that was great, because the area is full of stories – and, unlike many other parts of modern England, the people know them. All the inhabitants of Tadley know about the Tadley broomsquires and the Tadley treacle mines – and if I were to tell stories about them, we'd get a nice bit of to and fro banter going; the very stuff of storytelling.

I arrived in the area a couple of hours before the booking, because I fancied a wander around old Calleva Atrebatum, the site of that largely vanished Roman city. It was winter, so it was dark by five o'clock, but I thought that as the site was roughly rectangular, I couldn't get lost if I just walked around the perimeter.

I was wrong of course. Well, the path didn't just follow the rather more complicated than oblong shape, which was far larger than I'd anticipated, there were ancient stone walls going off in different directions, with paths cutting off at right angles, right angles that could be the corners of the site, or maybe not! When I finally got back onto a road, I had no idea where I was – or whether I was on the same side of Calleva Atrebatum as I'd left my car. Eventually a farmer gave me a lift to my car, which was all a bit embarrassing, and I did get to the storytelling venue in time. Just. Still, I had another story to tell.

I had been pixie-led, that wondrous phrase that describes more than just being lost – it describes the bafflement and bemusement of finding things not as they should be, of finding yourself unexpectedly back where you started from, or in the opposite direction from where you expected, or finding that when you thought you'd arrived in familiar territory, that the familiar had become unfamiliar, that directions were reversed, that here was there, and there was here.

But I also had a sense, as I blindly wandered Calleva Atrebatum in the darkness, that there was something else there, something very large, something that merged with the shadows.

Maybe it was the Giant Onion – not a giant onion, but a giant called Onion! The Giant Onion was reputed to live in the ruined city, scaring away anyone who entered by pulling ghastly faces at them. It was the Giant Onion who threw a stone at a mischievous imp who was taunting him, leaving the nearby Imp Stone next to the Silchester Road, a stone that clearly shows the indentation of a giant's thumb; and Roman coins found within the site were always known as 'Onion's Pennies'.

We always make giants comical in stories, but the presence I'd felt that evening wasn't at all comical. Then the 'pixie-led' stories started to come to me, the stories about disorientation and mystification. So …

Once upon a time there was a broomsquire from Tadley. One day he was heading homewards past Calleva Atrebatum, after selling his besoms at Hogwood, Swallowfield and Stratfield Saye. At the ruined arch, the entrance to the old city, sat a blind beggar. He was raggedy, smelly, and generally tatterdemalion. 'A penny, sir, an Onion penny for a poor, blind beggar.'

'Get away from me,' said the broomsquire, who was both repelled and fearful of anyone who should be sitting at the gates of Calleva Atrebatum.

'Just a penny, sir, a penny,' wheedled the beggar.

'I said get away from me,' shouted the broomsquire, and pushed the man. He hadn't meant to push him over, but he caught the beggar off balance, and the beggar tumbled down the embankment into a ditch.

'A curse on you,' shouted the beggar, 'a curse on you!'

It wasn't long before the broomsquire should have been approaching Tadley, but as he turned that familiar corner, all he saw ahead of him was Calleva Atrebatum. Once more he set off for Tadley, but just as Tadley should have come into view, with his own cottage, and his wife and children, there again was the crumbling gate to Calleva Atrebatum. Over and over again. His clothes became raggedy, his body became skeletal – till he was more raggedy than ever the blind beggar had been. This continued until one day the skeletal broomsquire toppled over, and fell into the same ditch into which he'd pushed the blind beggar.

As he lay there, the thought came to him, 'Today, I go home.' He hauled himself out of the ditch, knowing that this time he really was going to reach Tadley. When he rounded that old, familiar corner, there was his cottage, and outside it there was a crowd of people.

Some men came forward and told him to go away.

'What happens here?' asked the shocked broomsquire.

'Mind your own bloody business,' said the young man.

'Please, please tell me.'

'My mother, the woman of the house, is giving birth to my half-brother or sister.'

The broomsquire gawped at his grown-up son.

'But – I am your father, she is my wife.'

'That's a foul thing to say,' shouted the young man, 'my father was murdered by the Giant Onion twelve years ago – and the man who is with her is her second husband.'

The broomsquire tried to convince his son and the others, but eventually they drove him away.

So now his ghost stumbles around Calleva Atrebatum – a punishment, no doubt, for his lack of charity: something that makes me a bit nervous given that I didn't buy a copy of the *Big Issue* today from that bloke outside the corner shop.

So, maybe the ghost of the broomsquire stumbles around old Calleva Atrebatum – or maybe it's the blind beggar – or maybe the Giant Onion – or maybe some sort of a synthesis of all of them. These stories could all be some sort of a symbolic expression of an older story – for even King Arthur, that very personification of a multitude of ancient stories, is associated with the site; indeed Geoffrey of Monmouth claimed that Arthur was crowned there. Arthur is said to sleep under many a hill throughout Britain, including the appropriately named Sleeper's Hill in Winchester, so why shouldn't he slumber beneath Calleva Atrebatum? Maybe the giant is Arthur himself. But then, who is Arthur? (Now isn't that the title of multitudes of books sold in New Agey bookshops from Basingstoke to Brechin?) Is he a symbol of some sort of order, something that holds particular appeal during a time of doubt?

Or a god?

In 1866 archaeologists dug up a bronze eagle at Calleva Atrebatum. Rosemary Sutcliff, in her book *The Eagle of the North* – which became a Hollywood film – created a great story around the eagle, making it the mascot of a lost legion which disappeared into the Highlands of Scotland. Rosemary Sutcliff was, of course, a great storyteller, and had a talent for weaving tales around artefacts. I, however, am a purveyor of nothing but the naked truth, and can tell you that the eagle was part of a monumental sculpture. The eagle, you see, is the primary sacred animal of Jupiter, the god of gods, the Sky God. Maybe Jupiter, despised and abandoned god of the departed Romans, still stumbles around Calleva Atrebatum, a shadow of his former self, a god in reduced circumstances become a giant – a god reduced to gargoyle or ghost.

Maybe, one day, he'll go to Reading Museum and demand his eagle back.

13

Back to School

It was back in the 1960s.

A young woman from Basingstoke was about to get engaged to a young man from Farnborough, and much of their courtship was carried out with the aid of a Royal Enfield motorcycle. She was looking forward to his arrival at her house on the outskirts of Basingstoke, because that Saturday they were due to head southwards down the old Roman road to posh old Winchester, to buy the ring.

On the previous Friday evening they'd gone to the pictures in Basingstoke, and after he'd taken her home, he headed back towards Farnborough in a downpour of rain; a truly filthy, horrible night. Riding along Galley Hill Road in Church Crookham, he hit a patch of oil, skidded, and came off his bike. He died next to the churchyard. Maybe if he'd been wearing a helmet – and he did have one – things would have been different, but this was the sixties.

The young woman knew nothing about this, so the next morning she eagerly awaited his arrival, and the trip to Winchester.

The doorbell rang and she opened the door – there was no one there.

He was just down the road, revving up the bike, wearing a helmet and a scarf covering most of his face. What she could see of his face looked very pale.

'You all right?'

'Get on,' he said tersely. She donned her leather jacket, and climbed on pillion.

Gazing at the back of his helmet something didn't seem right – then she realised that he wasn't taking the Winchester Road, he was heading the opposite way, out towards Hook and Farnborough.

'What are you doing?' she shouted, but her words were lost in the wind and the roar of the bike. Then she saw that there was blood running down his neck from the back of his helmet, and something that looked horribly like brains.

She started to scream as he stopped the bike in Galley Hill Road, and dragged her into Christ Church graveyard. There was a spade leaning against the church wall, and he grabbed it and started to dig. She kept trying to run, but every time he grabbed her and dragged her back to the side of the deepening grave – however, when he was waist deep in the ground, she broke free and ran – through the porch, and into the church. Desperately she hauled on the bell rope – and that's how the vicar found her, hauling on the bell rope and crying hysterically.

Now this is an old, old story. Folklorists have given story types categorisations and numbers, sounding remarkably like food additives, and, according to the Thompson motif-index of folk literature, this is E215! The last version I came across was in Iceland, and involved a dead minister carry-ing his intended bride away on a horse. But I heard this story from teenagers at a secondary school in the Aldershot/Farnborough conurbation, and they knew nothing of motif-indexes, or obscure books about folklore; they were just telling a horror story. (It was over ten years ago that I heard this, so some of the details might be adapted, but I think I've got the gist of it.) These teenagers were being genuine tradi-tion bearers, the more so for being unaware of it.

Kids and schools are great sources of traditional folklore. 'Bloody Mary' in the school toilets is a regular source of fear; no doubt that's where J.K. Rowling got the idea for Moaning Myrtle.

On one occasion I was even asked to tell stories in a primary school in order to dispel belief in this particular myth. The big kids, the Year 6s, had been frightening the infants with tales of Bloody Mary, and it had all got a bit out of control.

Imagine: there's a primary school classroom, buzzing with life and colour and activity – and then there's the toilets, stinky and echoing, gurgling and rattling noises emanating from the plumbing. It's scary. Infants at this particular school were refusing to go for a wee, when they desperately wanted to do so, and some of them were even getting constipated, because who would ever poo in the malign presence of Bloody Mary?

My task was to 'deconstruct' the stories, so the younger children could see that it wasn't real (the head teacher's task was to give those Year 6s a right royal rollicking!), but it all demonstrated the power of the imagination. Teachers often seek to stimulate children's imaginations in the hope of getting them writing, but they don't want this. And those Year 6s effectively demonstrated the power of storytelling, but not in a way the teachers would want!

But it isn't just the children who tell stories about ghosts in schools. The caretaker of one school told me that he'd left a bucket of water and container of bleach in one toilet, whilst he was cleaning another, and whilst he did so something hurled the bleach into the bucket so hard that it splashed the ceiling. I, of course, put on my cynical voice and said, 'Well, it just fell in.'

'No,' he said, and told me that it went in so hard that it was propelled by more than gravity. I'd better not say the name of the school, but let's just say that when I looked into the story afterwards, I discovered that lines of monks supposedly walk through the place where the school toilets were later situated. These places, though, can work on the imaginations of adults just as much as on the imaginations of children. I'm sure that part of this is that when a school is in full function, there's so much life, drama and activity going on, that the contrast, after the kids have gone, is so quiet that it seems eerie.

Cleaners at Mount Pleasant School, a classic Victorian school building in Southampton, have told me that they never liked to be the last one on the premises – because they were liable to hear echoes of the past; the slamming of the lids of old-fashioned desks – even the drone of bombers passing overhead during the Blitz.

And then there are the ghosts of children themselves, and a lonely ghost upon a hill.

St Catherine's Hill overlooks Winchester, and on top of the hill there is a 'miz-maze'. There are two miz-mazes in Hampshire, one at Breamore and this one, next to Winchester. They aren't hedged mazes, they are ridge and furrow patterns cut into the ground. These aren't play-grounds where you can enjoy the sensation of being lost in a giant puzzle, they seem to represent some act of penance or self-flagellating worship – a place where people shuffle along on their knees; a task, certainly not a pleasure.

Winchester dog walkers tell of how, in the early morning, or at dusk, they can hear weeping from the miz-maze, and whilst they can see nothing, they can sense a boy shuffling around and around.

The story is that the ghost is a former pupil of Winchester College, the public school at the bottom of the hill, and that having committed some sort of misdemeanour, his punishment was not being allowed to go home for the Whitsun holidays. He spent the time up on the hill, re-digging the ancient miz-maze, of which little remained but marks on the ground. Obsessively he continued his task till his heart burst, and he died at the centre of the maze.

And that's one of the saddest stories I know – the boy being trained to become one of the distorted administrators of this wondrous and benighted country, symbolising all of the powerful with his powerlessness; his continuous shuffling and circling of the hill.

Some motherly figure – please go up there and set him free!

14

DAVEY JONES' LOCKER

I used to go once a week to a lovely school called St John's Primary, in Gosport – a school switched on enough to take advantage of an arts partnership scheme. Sometimes at lunchtime I'd take a wander, in order to eat my sandwiches outside – I'd cross the road, walk through the park, and find myself on the edge of Gosport Creek.

Muddy, tidal, with a rotting wooden boat half sunk in the mud, one of those fascinating, unmanaged areas; and then across the narrow gap of Portsmouth Harbour there was Pompey, and the Spinnaker Tower, the masts of the *Victory*, and the roofs of the naval dockyard. One lunchtime I gazed across the creek after one of those cold, clammy mists had rolled in from the sea, and the top of the Spinnaker Tower hovered above the mist, whilst the seabirds cried mournfully as they flew in from the Solent.

Naturally enough Gosport Creek became part of many of the children's inner landscape – and their stories expanded the creek into another world, a very maritime world peopled with pirates, smugglers, sea monsters and even mermaids, although I thought that a Gosport mermaid might well be one that sits on a rock, smoking a roll-up, and telling everyone to f*** off (not that I suggested that to the children, I hasten to add; their mermaids tended to be more like Ariel, from the Disney film).

But then, Gosport is full of ghost stories – and how could it be otherwise? Think of all those ships that have sailed out of Gosport; think of its position on the other side of the lagoon from old Pompey – which makes it in some ways an extension of Portsmouth, connected by the Gosport Ferry. And there's the narrow gap, between Gosport Town and Portsmouth Dockyard, through which all those ships glide – and at one time the gibbeted remains of Jack the Painter dangled from Fort Blockhouse, which lies in the gap, as a warning to sailors not to indulge in mutinous or revolutionary behaviour.

Whose corpse by ponderous irons wrung
High up on Blockhouse Beach was hung,
And long to every tempest swung?
Why truly, Jack the Painter.
                – Henry Slight, 1820

… but you'll have to read *Hampshire and the Isle of Wight Folk Tales* for that story!

And the submarines – now that's something to provide hauntings, especially in those days of diesel and shale, when the submarines sailed from Gosport. Cyril Tawney, folk singer and ex-submariner, sang about this:

On the 5th of November in '53
The big man at Dolphin, he sent for me
'We brought you here, sonny, 'cause we want you to know
We've booked you a berth in water below'.

With the diesel and shale, diesel and shale
We've booked you a berth with the diesel and shale.

But when I protested, 'I'm no volunteer'
They said 'we ain't had one in many's a year
But that's a wee secret between you and me
There's many a pressed man down under the sea'.

With the diesel and shale, diesel and shale
Down under the sea with the diesel and shale.

In 1951 HM Submarine *Affray* was lost, mysteriously, after she'd dived in the Solent, and it is surely the *Affray* that is the shadowy, spectral submarine that is sometimes seen gliding up Gosport Creek, the captain standing on the conning tower, peering out from another world.

And then there are the pubs. Gosport has got more than its fair share of haunted boozers, as it has more than its fair share of pubs anyway – even in these desperate times of pub closures – and there was a time when the public house was a thriving centre of activity; and a frightening place for a simple country man. Which brings me to a story.

Once upon a time – a Napoleonic, Nelsonian sort of a time – an early nineteenth century sort of a time, there was a farmer who lived next to Sandy Lane, near remote and obscure Shedfield.

The navy had been blockading the Channel for some time, and when it came into Portsmouth there was a great call for beef – which could be salted for rations. Word had reached the farmer that he could take his cattle to Gosport, and they'd fetch a good price from the navy victuallers.

So he walked his cattle down through Shedfield, Wickham and Fareham, and indeed he did get a good price – the effects of what felt like perpetual war with the French weren't good for agriculture – but at least here was an advantage.

With that money in his pocket he should have headed straight back to Shedfield and old Sandy Lane, but the bustle, the light, the drunken roarings and the screechings of the Gosport Nans – it was all too exotic to him, and he just had to take a look. Just a quick one.

It soon got round the tavern that he had money in his pocket – and didn't he suddenly seem to have so many friends? He knew he should leave, tear himself away from this mayhem – but there was another arm around his shoulders, a female voice in his ear – and the world was becoming blurry.

Then there was a crashing, a banging, and a shouting, and the clientele of the pub scattered.

'Here's a fine one for you, my lovely boys,' said the landlady – who not five minutes ago had been whispering in the farmer's ear.

The bosun's mate, who was leading the press gang, seized the farmer by the arm; so the farmer took a lumbering, ineffectual swing at the bosun's mate – which resulted in him receiving a rain of blows and a crack on the back of the head from a cudgel.

He woke up, and wished he hadn't, on board ship – and this wasn't just any ship, this was the flagship of the fleet, under the command of Captain Hardy, and carrying Admiral Lord Nelson himself; this was HMS *Victory*.

Of course he had to 'learn the ropes', and he was more capable of doing this than many. He was a farmer, a landsman – but he was strong and used to hardship, and he could fight for the space to hang his hammock, or fight for his share of the rations as well as any bugger else. He survived. That is, up until the Battle of Trafalgar.

Nelson got word that the French and Spanish fleet were off Cape Trafalgar, and in the October of 1805 that is where the two fleets met. There have been lots of pictures made of that particular encounter; paintings, drawings, engravings. Some of them seem merely picturesque, whilst others give more of an impression of the horrors of war, but all of them are pictures of the battle on the surface of the sea.

But what about below the surface? Cannon balls, chains, blocks and tackles, masts, spars; shattered fragments all raining down to the bottom of the sea. And bodies. Bits of body, limbs and torsos, and whole spread-eagled corpses, arms outstretched like starfish – all raining down through the silent water, after the eardrum-shattering blast and cannonade of the world above.

And one of those starfish corpses was the farmer – blown from the ship during the height of battle – never more to see the fields of Shedfield, or old Sandy Lane in June all lined with elderflower, bubbling like foam.

Well, Gosport and Portsmouth were in great spirits when news of the victory got back to England – and to be honest the death of Nelson didn't lessen these high spirits; it just gave a perfect opportunity to indulge in drunken, maudlin lamenting – and that is something really pleasurable.

The sailors got back with their prize money – and there was Nelson's body in a brandy cask – and everyone saw 'Hearts of Oaks' as heroes, and Britannia ruled the waves.

The sailor who put his arms around the landlady of a particular tavern in Gosport was somehow familiar to her, but she'd seen many a sailor pass through her establishment, and she'd sold a good few farmers and fools to the press gang. He had a livid scar across his face which seemed to have shifted his features around a bit, anyway. What he had that attracted her was, of course, money – and he had lots of it. He ordered food and drink, and drink and food, and he wanted her to join him in the feast – not with the rest of the carousing rabble, not even in the snug – but in a separate room she had upstairs. He had enough money to make that worthwhile, even if he was an ugly bastard.

Now I don't know exactly what he ordered, but here, culled from James Cramer's *Book of Portsmouth*, is an item-ised bill that was presented to a couple of sailors at one of the public houses in Point – that is old Spice Island in Portsmouth – in 1807, and it tells you something about the appetites of sailors when they were in the money:

40 pots of beer – 20s
18½ pints of gin – 18s
8 glasses of gin – 2s
Oysters – 4s
Shrimps – 2s
20 pots of porter – 10s
7 noggins of gin and peppermint – 7s
1 quart of rum – 7s
6 noggins of rum – 3s
10 noggins of gin – 5s
Breakfast – 6s
Pears and apples – 2s 6d
Lodgings – 5s
7½ pints of gin – 7s
20 pots of beer – 10s
10 half-noggins of beer – 5s
Attendance – 2s 6d
            Total £5 14s

After they'd gorged themselves, he took her by the arm and said, 'Come with me' and he opened a door in a wall that had never had a door, and she couldn't resist, she felt compelled to follow him down a dank, dripping corridor. And hell wasn't all fire and brimstone, though he'd seen something of that before the sea took his shattered body, it was dark and wet and cold, and Davey Jones was dancing a slow hornpipe in time to the movement of the sea.

And the landlady was never seen again.

As the farmer had done what he had returned to the land of the living to do, his ghost is presumably not one of Gosport's more persistent haunters – but you still have to be careful if you're out on the booze in Gosport. There's always someone to take you by the hand and lead you straight to hell.

15

THE DESOLATION OF FRANCHEVILLE

When visitors go to the Isle of Wight, they might go to Shanklin, or Alum Bay, or one of the theme parks – and why not? They're great places to take the kids. Or they might want to go on a ghost walk and stand outside the gates of Knighton Gorges in the darkness. If they fancy going upmarket they might go to Cowes in order to float around in a yacht whilst wearing very expensive marine clothing.

But visitors don't so often wander along the rural north coast outside of Cowes, the coast facing the mainland, and I think they're missing something.

I'm particularly fond of the area around Newtown. Newtown is a hamlet that once upon a time was a thriving port called Francheville; a town hall stands in splendid and strange isolation, and down the road there is a building that was once a pub, and is always referred to as Noah's Ark. To add to this air of strangeness Newtown has its own Pied Piper legend, one which W.H. Auden claimed was the original, which got pinched by Robert Browning and transposed to Hamelin! Francheville's Pied Piper led the rats out to the mudflats in the old harbour, where they stuck fast whilst the tide came in and drowned them. I think those mudflats are wondrous, an inter-tidal area which has its own appearing and disappearing ecosystem – now you see it, now you don't. Now it adapts to being submerged and to absorbing the richness of the sea, now it faces the air, the sun, and the sky.

There's a ghost there as well, though some people call her a mermaid. She has long white hair, and she drifts the inter-tidal zone looking for her baby. When the tide is in, however, she holds her baby in her arms, and melts into the sunset. That is, of course, if the sunset and the high tide happen to coincide.

The area has seen horrors. It is possible that the Anglo-Saxon King of Wessex, Caedwalla, carried out a policy of 'ethnic cleansing' against the Jutes – that must leave ghosts. Then, there is evidence that the Danes attacked Francheville in 1001; these small coastal ports were always vulnerable. Then later, the then prosperous town of Francheville with its oyster beds, and its Gold Street and Silver Street, was struck by the plague, and if this wasn't enough, the French attacked in 1377 and destroyed the place. The Pied Piper legend claims that there were no young fighting men to take on the French, because the piper had lured them all away as children.

So maybe the time when the fisherman lived in a rickety-rackety hut on the Francheville shore was in the time of the Jutes, or the time of the French raid, or a once upon a time – I wouldn't know. But what I do know is that he was all alone.

He'd trail his nets in the Solent and he'd see beautiful sights. Sometimes, in those days, he'd see the tail fin of a whale as it dived down into the world beneath the sea, sometimes he'd see flocks of birds fly in shifting shapes from the shore and perform their own aerial dance between the two coasts, sometimes he'd see the sun setting over the water and everything would turn red; the sky would be red, the sea would be red, the clouds would be red.

But he had no one to share this with. He'd return to shore, sell some fish, trade some fish, eat some fish – but there was no one with whom to share his experiences.

One day he'd just had enough, so he hauled in his nets and threw them into the bottom of the boat, he lowered the sail, and threw it into the bottom of the boat – and then he just sat there. Like a big turnip.

For three days he floated and drifted – and at the end of that time a great moon rose out of the sea, and out of the shimmering moonlight came the Queen from under the Sea, with her comb, her mirror and her eyes of aquamarine.

'What are you doing, just floating on my waters?' she demanded.

'I just don't care anymore,' he said. 'I've got no one to share anything with, and I don't care.'

'Well,' said she, 'for three days and three nights you've left my fish alone, and so I feel sorry for you. Hoist your sail, sail for home, and see what awaits you.'

And so, without reflecting on whether mermaids with eyes of precious stones have the capacity for sympathy, he sailed for home.

When he got back to his rickety-rackety wooden hut, on the muddy old shore of Francheville, there was a young woman. She was a bit scruffy, and a bit scrawny, she wasn't very clean, her hair stuck out in all directions, and her clothes were raggedy.

'Who are you?' he said.

'My mother and father have died,' she replied, 'and I'm all alone in the world, so I've come to share my life with you, and you to share your life with me.'

And the fisherman, instead of being grateful for no longer being alone, thought to himself, 'If the Queen from under the Sea was going to send me a wife, you'd think she'd send me a princess, all dressed in fine clothes, and with fine jewellery – but not this – this scruffy girl.'

But they were married, because strange things happen in stories, just as they do in life, and they had a baby son.

Every day the fisherman would go out fishing, and when he returned his wife would tell him stories. They were always stories of the sea – stories of shoals of fish swimming in the bottle green waters off Spithead and Hurst, tales of ancient, drowned churches and villages, stories of the magic islands beyond the horizon, and stories of the world of the Queen from under the Sea. He loved those stories, and one day he said to her, 'I want you to take me there.'

'Where?'

'To the world of the Queen from under the Sea of course; I want you to take me there.'

'Don't be silly, that's only a story.'

'No it isn't, it's real – and you were sent to me by the Queen from under the Sea – so you should be a princess, and I should be a prince. I want you to take me to the world under the sea.'

'I can't,' she cried, 'I can't.'

'Then get out of here – GET OUT AND DON'T COME BACK, not until you're ready to take me to the world under the sea.'

And so – before he regretted his hasty words – she left, and she walked all the way to Alum Bay, and that night she lay down by the sea, with her baby in her arms, and fell asleep.

And when she awoke, the baby was gone.

'Where's the baby? Where's the baby?' she cried, and she ran up and down the shoreline calling for the baby, but the baby was gone.

And her hair, which had been black, turned white with grief.

And they said that the baby had gone to the world of the Queen from under the Sea, and surely she could have gone back there too. But the story is that a white-haired woman, returned from Alum Bay, can be seen floating up and down the mudflats beyond Newtown, that once was Francheville, and she's calling for her baby. Maybe the haunting is some sort of an imprint; a recalling of a past event.

As for the fisherman, he turned his back on the Island, and old Francheville, and swam out to sea, and as he did so he turned into a sea creature himself. He swam till he reached Southampton Water, and still he continued to swim, up the River Test and on and on, till the river became small, and still this strange sea creature flapped along the stream, its heart bursting. It came to the source of the River Test at Ashe, and still it flapped over damp meadows, and through hedgerows and nettle beds, and bramble bushes, until it came to Highclere. At Highclere the sea creature dragged itself up an ancient yew tree in the churchyard, and sat there barking and grunting at the locals.

And this is one of the most unlikely legends of Hampshire, indeed one of the oddest in England. A Grampus, a strange dolphin-like sea creature, sat in a tree, in inland Hampshire, and it sat there until it was banished to the Red Sea by a local cleric. But that's the legend; and indeed the whole story is most peculiar.

16

THE MISTLETOE BRIDE

When I wrote *Hampshire and the Isle of Wight Folk Tales* I thought I'd better include most of Hampshire's more well-known folk tales, because if I didn't someone was sure to lurch up to me at some event where I was telling stories, and announce loudly, 'I'm surprised you didn't include the story of (so and so). Don't you know it?'

This is generally a fate worth avoiding; especially as such a person is out to score points, not to happily share a story.

However, there was one well-known story I didn't include (and yes, this has been pointed out to me) and that's because I really didn't like the story, it made me feel claustrophobic. It's the story that is sometimes called the Mistletoe Bough, sometimes the Mistletoe Bride. I have recently, however, come to realise that there's more to the story than I discerned, something that takes away from the claustrophobia, so I think, maybe, I'm ready to tell it.

Firstly, however, the bare bones of the usual presentation.

Once upon a time the young tenant of Marwell Hall, near Owlsebury, was betrothed to a young woman of good family, and they were due to have a Christmas wedding. After the ceremony, all in high spirits, they decided to have a game of hide and seek. The bride found her way into an unused and deserted part of the great house, saw an old oak chest, and decided to hide in it. When she shut the lid, a lock snapped shut – and she was trapped. The wedding guests searched Marwell Hall from top to bottom, and some of them must have walked past the chest – but inside it, she suffocated.

It was many years later that someone prised the chest open to find therein the mouldering remains of the young bride. Since then her ghost has walked the corridors of Marwell Hall, and her hands are bleeding claws.

Well, like many stories, this tale has many locations; in Hampshire it is also located at Bramshill House near Eversley, but it is also located at other grand houses through-out Britain. It would seem to be derived from a poem by the popular Victorian 'parlour poet' Thomas Haynes Bayley, a poem that Bayley based on an Italian story, and which was put to music by Sir Henry Bishop, composer of 'Home Sweet Home'. At Christmas time Victorian patriarchs could stand at the head of the parlour, and sing the ballad in a mournful and stentorian voice – something infinitely prefer-able to having to watch a Disney film on the telly.

So all these grand houses could adopt the story, and come to believe that it had been part of their traditional history for hundreds of years – but there was something different going on at Marwell Hall.

Firstly, it already specialised in the ghosts of trapped women – and the invidious effects of arranged marriage.

For a while, the tenants of Marwell Hall were the Seymours, whose daughter Jane had caught the eye of Henry VIII. It is said that King Henry waited at Marwell Hall to hear the news that his previous wife, Anne Boleyn, had been executed, so he could then be betrothed to Jane. Therefore the ghost of that trapped woman, Anne Boleyn, is said to walk the hall, with her head tucked underneath her arm, in order to lay her vengeful curse upon the Seymours. But then it would be hard to be more trapped than poor Jane Seymour, whose motto as queen was 'Bound to obey and serve', and who died giving birth to the future king, Edward VI. That poor motherless boy was put on the throne at the age of nine, and was therefore, until his early death, surrounded by perpetual intrigue and political manoeuvring.

So the ghost of Jane Seymour is also said to walk the corridors of Marwell Hall – and, clearly, both of these women lived in metaphorical boxes. But, enough of gloom, enough of claustrophobia, enough of pale ghosts wandering interminable corridors. There is another story.

Firstly – the ghost.

Is it a ghost?

When is a ghost not a ghost?

If you walk the banks of the River Itchen, near Ovington and Lovington Lane, Couch Green and Martyr Worthy, you might see a host of fairy ladies riding on white horses, and at their head a stately lady with a great hawk upon her glove. She is the Queen under the Hill – but when she was mortal she was betrothed to the tenant of Marwell Hall, and there was no arguing against that.

As a child and a young teenager she had the freedom of the woods and fields and high, airy Downs above Winchester

– but then came the time for family duty; for arrangements and social positioning, for the selling, trading and bartering of daughters.

In her land of woods and fields, however, she had already met the King under the Hill, who rode upon a goat from his halls beneath the Downs.

So, when after a marriage ceremony as hollow as the hollow hills, the nobles, notables, notaries, noggins and noodles agreed to indulge in her hide-and-seek frolic, her farewell to those carefree years, she ran three times widdershins (anti-clockwise) around Marwell Hall, and then disappeared off to meet the King under the Hill, him with his glittering eyes and a-riding on a goat.

She was never found, and so they concocted a story that somehow, by some subconscious process, reflected the very entrapment that she escaped. Then, centuries later, it all merged into a Victorian Christmas song.

The lands of Marwell Hall are now an open, spacious and humane zoo with a commitment to conservation. No doubt the ghost of Victor the giraffe haunts the place, because he, poor creature, did the splits in 1977, possibly whilst attempting to pay attention to a female giraffe called Dribbles. Despite all attempts to get him back on his feet, using a sling made by soft-hearted and empathic Portsmouth dockyard workers, he died in that position, his relationship with Dribbles sadly unconsummated. Possibly his ghost, floating around legs akimbo, still haunts the place.

And as for the Queen under the Hill, well, if she's not gone, she lives there still … although she and the King must have been mightily angered when a huge motorway cutting was hacked through Twyford Down, the very centre of their domain. You may be reminded of her presence if you're driving north along the M3 in the evening. Watch as you come to the two slip roads that head off to the A3090 and the B3335 – you'll see, ahead of you, the glittering imprint of the Queen under the Hill clearly in the landscape, the slip roads being her arms. When you've seen her once, you'll see her every time.

But I don't know if you could call that a ghost.

17

THE RAT KING

You are never more than six feet away from a rat.

That's the old adage, anyway, though how anyone could possibly know is beyond me. More than six feet beyond me. But there are always rats somewhere nearby – and sometimes the eye attunes to them and suddenly they seem to be everywhere.

One time I was walking along a mundane paving-slabbed pathway, through council shrub beds, in a very late twentieth-century part of Basingstoke, and I wondered why there seemed to be such rippling movement from within the shrubs, like an ocular migraine, almost hallucinatory. I stopped, my eyes attuned, and then I could see that the shrub beds were swarming with rats, Pied Piper masses of rats, with people strolling through, blithely unaware of the ratty host around them.

Then, in the countryside, in gardens, in parks, in graveyards there are those perfectly round rat holes that look somehow sinister, because we think rats are sinister. Maybe that is because of the bubonic plague, or rat-bite fever, or Weil's disease. Or maybe it's because of those bulbous tails – I confess I have an aversion to them – and given that squirrels are pretty similar to rats, it feels hardly fair to have no enmity towards them simply because they have bushy tails. Then maybe it's because rats steal our food – nibble nibble

nibble – the grain in the granary – nibble nibble nibble – the bread in the bakery – nibble nibble nibble – the leftovers from the plate. Serves you right for wasting food.

I expect that rats think humans are a bigger nuisance. Don't we swarm more than any rats? Don't we carry much more disease? Aren't we even more repulsive? Instead of pink tails, we're all pink and hairless. But then – they need us. They live off us. They eat our food and live in, around and under our buildings – and they do it wild; without the sycophancy of cats and dogs.

Minstead is a lovely place, and I would certainly never accuse it of being rat infested – not any more than anywhere else anyway. I saw one cottage there advertised as a place to come 'to get away from the rat race', to leave the corporate rats of London town and come and dwell in Arcadian bliss. Presumably complete with Internet connection.

And it's got a great pub, the Trusty Servant, with its singular sign showing a man, a servant, and a pig's head.

And All Saints church with its house-like windows, and enclosed room so that no one could see whether the family from Castle Malwood House were listening to the sermon or playing cards, and a separate fireplace for that room, so that maybe the family members could cluster round it and drink sloe gin, whilst the poor people amongst the rest of the congregation shivered in the gallery and listened to the vicar droning on from the top of the most wondrous and strange three-decker pulpit. Of course, that's the past, and when one Christmas day family members and I wandered in for the Christmas service, we were made most welcome, and the female vicar conducted a service that was warm and meaningful.

I have seen rat holes in the churchyard though – but then you get them everywhere, I've seen them in my own back garden.

And then there are the stories about rat lines – they were told about the forest. Rats who are resettling from one place to another are reputed to travel in straight lines, like Roman roads, led by their king. Nothing will make them deviate from that line; should there be a sleeping creature in their path, well – nibble nibble nibble, crunch crunch crunch – there'll be nothing left. In the 1930s, when the byways and footpaths were full of tramping men, and some women, stories were told of unfortunate souls being consumed after they unwittingly found a sleeping place in the path of a rat line.

But the story I'm about to tell goes back two centuries before that – and it tells of a time when a farmer near Minstead liked to exercise his cruelty on captured rats. Well, he mostly liked to exercise his cruelty on other people, on his wife, his children, and the peasants who worked his land. He was mean and vindictive, and because he liked to believe that he was always the victim and that people were always out to cheat him, he treated all others as enemies.

In his barn there were rat traps, and why wouldn't there be? No farmer wanted his grain to be eaten by rats, so he would put out rat traps, and quickly dispatch any rats they caught. Except this farmer didn't kill them quickly – he'd torture them. He'd poke them, he'd prod them; sometimes he'd burn them with smouldering charcoal.

On one occasion the farm workers saw that he had captured a particularly large rat – then they saw him go off and return with a squirming, wriggling sack over his shoulder. He tipped up the sack, and out tumbled a flurry of farm cats. The cats proceeded to stalk around and around the trap whilst the rat, frenzied with fear, looked almost demoniacal – it gibbered and squeaked, it foamed at the mouth, it wriggled and squirmed in the trap. The farm workers watched in horror, but it wasn't the sight of the rat that filled them with horror, it was the sight of the farmer's face. His normally sour features were now fixed into a hideous grin, his eyes shone, and he rubbed his hands together with hellish glee. Then he leaned forward and slowly lifted the trap door. The rat squeezed itself underneath and tried to make a dash for it, but the cats were on it in a hissing ball of fur, and then its tail could be seen, being gulped down the throat of a big ginger tom.

One harvest time Sunday morning, all the folk of the farm were in All Saints listening to the vicar holding forth from the top level of that extraordinary pulpit. The farmer had cursed God, folk, and their idle time off during the harvest, and, in a particularly foul mood, he had decided not to attend the service — quite an act of defiant blasphemy in those days. He inspected the barn, where the threshing and winnowing had been taking place, expecting to find fault with something. Then he looked up at the old wooden beams, and he froze, rigid with horror.

It was the Rat King.

The Rat King wasn't a giant rodent, or a rat wearing a crown.

The Rat King was a wheel.

Let me explain.

A Rat King is a mass of rats whose tails have become intertwined and stuck together, and then, according to the stories, the rats grow into each other and form a terrible, squeaking, gibbering wheel. The Rat King had been bowling along at the head of a rat line as a mighty colony of rats abandoned the forest village of Nomansland, on the border between Hampshire and the mad moon-raking county of Wiltshire, and headed for the more verdant pastures of Minstead.

And the farmer stood directly in the path of the rat line; whilst on the beam the Rat King glared at him with 101 eyes (one of his constituent parts only had one eye) – and then the line of rats came marching up the staddle stones, and spread out, coming in through the door, and between the planking – and they were on him. If you'd been there, and I'm glad *I* wasn't, what would you have seen, but a pink, wriggling mass of rats' tails, and a Rat King bowling around like a Catherine Wheel that celebrated Guy Fawkes Day on it true anterior date: Halloween.

When the farm folk got back from church, and when they looked into the barn, they called upon all of the saints of All Saints, for what did they see but a bloody, red skeleton; and out of the right eye socket – the flick of a rat's tail.

So now, somewhere below Lower Canterton, which is above Upper Canterton, walking through Piper's Wood, for the Pied Piper never got as far as Minstead, is the most terrible ghost; a stumbling skeleton festooned with rats' tails. I've never seen it myself, and I've never even met a bloke who knows a bloke who knows a bloke who has seen it – but then who'd go walking in Piper's Wood at midnight?

Anyway, the rat line reached Minstead and the village was infested. The locals had never heard of the Pied Piper, and he was either over on the Isle of Wight, off in Germany, or stuck in Piper's Wood anyway. So they brought in cats, and the rats ate the cats; they brought in dogs, and the rats ate the dogs; they fetched rat catchers, and they all gave up in the face of overwhelming odds.

Given that prayers in All Saints had no effect, and the vicar said (whilst the rats treated the pulpit as a helter-skelter) that it was a punishment for sinfulness (though the inhabitants of Minstead couldn't think that they'd really sinned any more than anyone else – chance would be a fine thing – and they were never as bad as the devilish inhabitants of Totton), the good folk of Minstead decided to take their problem to the great and mighty. Thus a deputation set off through the forest to visit Old John, 2nd Duke of Montagu, at his grand, stately pile in Beaulieu.

He suggested that they get cats.

They told him they had.

He suggested that they get dogs.

They told him they had.

He suggested that they employ rat catchers.

They told him they had.

He suggested that they pray.

They told him they had.

Now Old John wasn't such a bad duke, as dukes go, and he had never considered himself to be above the ways and whiles of common folk. He had a soft spot for Old Widow Dore, who Mr Brand the antiquary tells us was a parochial witch who had just been released from Winchester Prison, and he let her live in one of his houses, down by the mill. He visited her now and again to get potions and spells to counteract the various ailments of advancing age. The Reverend Richard Warner wrote in his excellent and frequently read *Topographical Remarks relating to South-Western parts of Hampshire*, 1793, that she was no 'black and midnight hag' but that her 'spells were chiefly used for the purpose of self-extrication in situations of danger' – and wouldn't that often be the purpose of spells for a vulnerable old woman; her only defence against a cruel world? But Old John wasn't cruel, and he valued her potions, and he thought that maybe she could do something to help the benighted inhabitants of Minstead.

So, after the Minstead deputation had started to trudge disconsolately back to their rat-infested home, he went to visit Old Widow Dore. Now, the Reverend Warner tells us that 'I have conversed with a rustic whose father had seen the old lady convert herself more than once into the form of a hare, or cat, when likely to be apprehended in wood-stealing, to which she was somewhat addicted'. Addiction seems a strange word to describe the gathering of life's necessities! Anyway, on the promise of a supply of firewood that would see her to the end of her days, the Widow Dore transformed herself into the form of a cat, and sallied forth to Minstead. En route, she conversed with the fairisies and the sprites (they abound in the forest), and it was a combination of these beings that wiffled into Minstead, and drove out the rats; who all packed their bags and headed for Basingstoke.

Maybe this accounts for Minstead's current ghosts. Go there; have a couple of pints in the Trusty Servant, and then look for the Adam and Eve oak trees, reputed to be two of the oldest trees in the Forest. If you look up at them as the sun sets, you might see the cat people – they could be fairisies, they could be cats, they could be ghosts. Whatever – they're another of the strange legends of the New Forest, and maybe they have something to do with the Widow Dore.

So there we are.

The rats are in the crypt.
The cats are in the graveyard.
The bats are in my belfry.

18

THE *TITANIC*:
A CAVALCADE
OF GHOSTS

One winter's night I was working late in Tower House, as I had a deadline to meet. Tower House is a medieval building situated next to the Archaeology Museum in Winkle Street, which used to be the town gaol so is quite a creepy place to be after dark. About 8 p.m., after hearing all sorts of noises which you often did in such an old building, like creaking floors, and falling bits of masonry from the old walls, I set the alarm and prepared to leave. I always used to open the door before I left and look up and down Winkle Street, to make sure the coast was clear, and to my shock I saw a ghost in the doorway of God's House Tower (the old archaeological museum), long flowing white robe blowing in the wind, and large black eyes. I shut the door and thought my eyes were playing tricks with me, as I had been working hard, but when I very gingerly opened them again I saw the red light of a cigarette tip …

This was written by my friend, Sheila Jemima – she was writing about old Southampton, the area I described in Chapter 6, and it's an area full of ghosts. The ghost that Sheila saw lit up a cigarette, because she turned out to be one of the town guides, about to take people on a ghost walk;

great fun. But maybe Sheila's brief moment of fear was a real ghostly experience, a true connection with the area – more authentic than the stories about to be told to the punters, as they followed their guide around old Southampton.

And so we march over plague pits, follow the course of twisted men who murdered fallen women, trot around battlefield sites, even put on armour and pretend to fight each other. It is comforting, therefore, to distance ourselves from the horror, to create 'Horrible Histories' and re-enactments, and package it for consumption. The ghosts are Halloween masks, and the history is a cherry-picked collection of clichés. And so, we edge forward through the shifting mists of our own ghosts in our villages, our towns, our cities; pick out certain events, certain major occurrences, and adopt them as specific symbols. Southampton chose as its symbol a specific event – the sinking of a ship, built in Belfast, 400 miles off the coast of Newfoundland.

It is a symbol that has become banal, the familiar picture of the great ship sliding into the water reproduced a million times, even reflected in the architecture of museums. But when that ship went down, she took with her whole sections of Southampton's population, so it's hardly surprising that it should create such a powerful memory in the city; though perhaps a bit more surprising that it should rate as the main tourist magnet.

But the event, the sinking, it is the city's main ghost, and why wouldn't it be? In 1912 whole streets in Northam, and the adjoining area, Chapel, dockland areas of Southampton, lost their menfolk when the *Titanic* went down. It is the tendency for writers, though, to trivialise this reality by pegging their obsessive theories to the event. Various conspiracy theories about the sinking include scurrilous stories about an upper-class man dressing as a woman in order to board a lifeboat, nonsense about cursed Egyptian mummies in the hold, and urban legends about the Belfast shipbuilder welded up in the hull. But wouldn't it be more dignified to remember the stokers, working-class men mostly from Southampton, who kept the fires burning till the last possible moment so electricity could be generated to keep the ship illuminated, or to remember the nurses who took children to safety, or to remember the people who passed the children through the crowd to the lifeboats?

If there are ghosts, and the ghosts are not tied to the Atlantic seabed, won't those ghosts be swirling through Southampton, up the meandering River Itchen?

There'll be plenty of other wraiths to join them, for death has always haunted Southampton. There was the complete sacking of the town in 1338, by French, Norman, Italian and Castilian raiders, who included in their number a pirate called Grimaldi, who used his plunder to found the state of Monaco. Then, in 1384, a galley, a death ship, glided into Southampton harbour from Marseilles, carrying the Black Death, the bubonic plague, into England. Of course there were scores of deaths soon after the *Titanic* disaster – the First World War and the subsequent influenza pandemic – and then the Blitz, the drone of bombers over Southampton, and the bombs raining down on the very inner-city areas that had supplied most of the *Titanic*'s crew.

So a huge multitude, a cavalcade of ghosts, can go swirling and whirling up the old river, led by the poor young cabin boy, Richard Parker from Itchen Ferry Village, who got eaten by his shipmates whilst adrift in an open boat. And this swirl of spectres congregate in the most haunted place in Southampton: underneath Northam Bridge.

I don't know if this place looks haunted, I rather think it does. To the tourist trade there is a certain cachet to medieval buildings, or old graveyards, or Tudor pubs – but that feeling of hauntedness comes from us, from our perceptions, not stone, timber or mortar. The present Northam Bridge was completed in 1954, and if you wander underneath it, by the western bank of the River Itchen, you see concrete and graffiti. But to me this place, where you stand and hear the drip drop of condensation into the river, and the Doppler effect of cars passing overhead like aeroplanes, holds the feel of somewhere ancient and significant – of the people paddling up the meandering river in the time of forest and settlement, and of the people drifting down it towards open sea.

And the story of the vanishing hitchhiker is often told of the road above your head, about how a girl hitches a lift from an elderly couple on a dark, wet, winter's evening, and of how she subsequently disappears, and the couple discover she'd died the previous year. It's a famous urban legend, but the significance lies in the choice of location – and in Southampton it is always set at Northam Bridge. And as I stand beneath the bridge I can imagine a similar story set there, when the last bridging point of the Itchen was way upriver at Mansbridge, and the ferryman, the Charon of the River Itchen, was transporting souls across to the Hades of Bitterne Manor, and a passenger vanished from his boat.

And spreading down the widening river from Northam Bridge, through the nineteenth and twentieth centuries, are the boatyards, the soap and candle works, the old margarine factory, the cement works, the wharves and hards, the pubs, the rows of terraced houses – the lives and loves, the jealousies and resentments, the joys and pleasures, the highs and lows.

And on the old maps, down by where Shamrock Quay was built at Millstone Point, in between Crabniton and Northam, there was the Hegestone, or Hagstone – possibly an old boundary marker. When my son and I wandered down there, on one cold Sunday morning in the 1980s, to the spot where the Hagstone would have been, we found the head and torso of a tailor's dummy, with glistening glass eyes.

Ghosts are, I imagine, what you make of them. The loss of the *Titanic* was a trauma for Southampton – at the same time it carried with it a whole group of circumstances that lead to mythologising. This was the maiden voyage of a great, and 'unsinkable', liner – so there is hubris. Then there is Thomas Hardy's 'Convergence of the Twain' – so there is inexorable fate. These are powerful elements of myth – things to make it seem more than a terrible historical accident.

So I'll leave the last words to the story of a woman who sailed on the *Titanic*, who survived, but who, every time a new *Titanic* film came out and they tried to drag her into the circus, made the point that there was a lot more to her life. She was the wonderfully named Mrs Winnifred Quick Van Tongerloo. Originally she was Winnie Quick from Plymouth, who, with her mum, travelled to Southampton and sailed on the *Titanic* as an eight-year-old girl emigrating to America (she later gained the Van Tongerloo part of her surname through marriage). She lived until 2002, but was never keen on being part of the furore, though demands were made on her after the films *A Night to Remember* in 1958, and *Titanic* in 1997. In the 1960s, Winnifred and her husband, Alois, travelled America in their station wagon; they visited every state except Hawaii. In spite of her fear of deep water, they once made the overnight crossing from Michigan to Wisconsin on the Ludington ferry. Her husband awoke during the night and found Winnifred was gone. He got up, and eventually found her standing by the railings on deck. A noise had awoken her in the night, and she'd been reminded of the *Titanic*, all those years ago. She had quietly got out of her bunk, so as not to awaken her husband, and went on deck to face her fears alone. It was a whisper, an old ghost, a part of her life.

And maybe that's what ghosts are – whispers of memory, thoughts of loss, fragments of lives, dreams, hopes, fears, the scar of trauma, noises in the night.

REFERENCES

Ash *et al* (ed.), Folklore, 'Myths and Legends of Britain' (*Readers Digest*, 1973)

Beddington, Winifred G. and Christy, Elsa B. (eds), *It Happened in Hampshire* (Hampshire Federation of Women's Institutes, Winchester, 1937)

Bell, Karl, 'Civic Spirits? Ghost Lore and Civic Narratives in Nineteenth Century Portsmouth' (unpublished article, University of Portsmouth, 2013)

Boase, Wendy, *The Folklore of Hampshire and the Isle of Wight* (B.T. Batsford Ltd, London, 1976)

Brand, John, Observations of Popular Antiquities Chiefly Understanding the Origin of Our Vulgar Country Ceremonies and Superstitions, Vol. II (F.C. & J. Rivington et al, London, 1815)

Elder, Abraham, *Tales and Legends of the Isle of Wight* (Simpkin, Marshall & Co. 1839)

Gillington, Alice, 'Wild Daffodils in the Wood', *Country Life*, 22 June 1912, pp. 927–28.

Jemima, Sheila (ed.), 'Chapel and Northam, an oral history of Southampton's Dockland Communities 1900–1945' (Southampton City Council, 1991)

Mann, John Edgar, *Hampshire Customs, Curiosities and Country Lore* (Ensign Publications, Southampton, 1994)

O'Donald Mays, James (ed.), *The New Forest Book: An Illustrated Anthology* (New Forest Leaves, Burley, 1989)

Thompson, Stith, *The Folktale* (University of California Press, 1977)

Vesey-Fitzgerald, Brian, *Hampshire and the Isle of Wight* (Robert Hale Ltd, London, 1949)

WEBSITES

Chapter 1

Valley mires, New Forest:

www.newforestlife.com/New_Forest_bog.html

www.newforestexplorersguide.co.uk/wildlife/habitats/valley-mires.html

www.newforestnpa.gov.uk/info/20087/beautiful_landscapes/204/heathland_and_mires/2

Chapter 3

Song about Clewer's Hill (near Sandy Lane), by the Bundell Brothers:

www.bundellbros.co.uk/clewershill.mp3

The Waltham Blacks:

www.exclassics.com/newgate/ng169.htm

Chapter 6

Henry Doman's poems:

www.amazon.com/Songs-Lymington-Henry-Doman/dp/B0068JCYDI

Account of the Groaning Tree by Jude James:

www.newforester.com/news/south-baddesleys-groaning-tree/

Chapter 7

Song, 'Beware Chalk Pit' by Graham Penny:

www.foresttracks.co.uk/folk_music_pages/folk_music_contraband.html

Chapter 17

The Minstead Cat people:

www.paranormaldatabase.com/reports/fairydata.php?pageNum_paradata=6&totalRows_paradata=250

Chapter 18

Mrs Winifred (Quick) Van Tongerloo:

www.titanichistoricalsociety.org/people/winnifred-van-tongerloo3.html

ABOUT THE AUTHOR

MICHAEL O'LEARY has been a professional storyteller since 1994, but he has been a storyteller since he learned to talk. Being a gardener, greenkeeper and teacher were all part of his apprenticeships and now he wanders the country telling stories in schools, prisons, hospitals, care homes, fêtes, festivals, museums, libraries, pubs and cocktail bars. He is the author of *Hampshire and Isle of Wight Folk Tales*, *Sussex Folk Tales* and *Hampshire and Isle of Wight Folk Tales for Children*, both with The History Press. He lives in Southampton.

Also from The History Press

HAUNTED

This series is sure to petrify everyone interested in the ghostly history of their hometown. Containing a terrifying collection of spine-chilling tales, from spooky sightings in pubs and theatres to paranormal investigations in cinemas and private homes, each book in the series is guaranteed to appeal to both serious ghost hunters and those who simply fancy a fright.

Find these titles and more at
www.thehistorypress.co.uk